NEW YORK CITY DOCS

*Hot-shot surgeons, taking the world by storm…
by day and by night!*

In the heart of New York City,
four friends sharing an apartment in Brooklyn are on
their way to becoming the best there is at the prestigious
West Manhattan Saints Hospital—and these driven docs
will let *nothing* stand in their way!

Meet Tessa, Kimberlyn, Holly and Sam
as they strive to save lives and become
top-notch surgeons in the Big Apple. Trained by
world-class experts, these young docs are the future—
and they're taking the medical world by storm.

But with all their time dedicated to patients,
late nights and long shifts, the last thing they expect
is to meet the loves of their lives!

For fast-paced drama and sizzling romance,
check out the

New York City Docs quartet:

Hot Doc from Her Past
Tina Beckett

Surgeons, Rivals…Lovers
Amalie Berlin

Falling at the Surgeon's Feet
Lucy Ryder

One Night in New York
Amy Ruttan

Available now!

Dear Reader,

I have a feeling that when grace and beauty were handed out I was either trying to sneak another serving of humour or I was off somewhere with my head in the clouds. Probably daydreaming about being swept off my feet by a hot hero… I've been swept off my feet, all right—by a dozen huge figurative and literal waves that I haven't seen coming simply because I'm a dreamer.

My heroine, Holly, is a dreamer too. She's grown up an awkward ugly duckling in a family of beautiful graceful swans and has had to learn to control her inner klutz. It hasn't been easy, and she tends to regress when she's flustered. And, boy, does Gabriel Alexander fluster her. So much so that it's pretty much a disaster waiting to happen—because Holly's about to go down for the count.

Gabriel's wrestling with his own demons. He recently lost the only family that mattered, and has just left a lucrative cosmetic surgery career in Hollywood to join the staff of a Manhattan teaching hospital. With his family's dysfunctional history, he's convinced that committed relationships aren't his thing. In fact families aren't his thing. He's better off alone.

But then the adorably klutzy Holly Buchanan literally falls at his feet, and soon it's Gabe who finds himself falling—hard and fast. She sends him reeling, tilting his world on its axis. But maybe he's always been off-centre and Holly has finally righted his world.

Since I'm a little klutzy myself, I must confess to having a soft spot for Holly. I hope you do too.

Happy reading!

Lucy

FALLING AT THE SURGEON'S FEET

BY
LUCY RYDER

First published in Great Britain 2015
by Mills & Boon, an imprint of Harlequin (UK) Limited,
Eton House, 18-24 Paradise Road, Richmond, Surrey, TW9 1SR

© 2015 Bev Riley

ISBN: 978-0-263-25880-6

After trying out everything from acting in musicals, singing opera, travelling and writing for a business newspaper, **Lucy Ryder** finally settled down to have a family and teach at a local community college, where she currently teaches English and Communication. However, she insists that writing is her first love, and time spent on it is more pleasure than work. She currently lives in South Africa, with her crazy dogs and two beautiful teenage daughters. When she's not driving her daughters around to their afternoon activities, cooking endless meals or officiating at swim meets, she can be found tapping away at her keyboard, weaving her wild imagination into hot romantic scenes.

Books by Lucy Ryder

Mills & Boon® Romance Medical Romance™

Resisting Her Rebel Hero
Tamed by Her Army Doc's Touch

**Visit the author profile page at
millsandboon.co.uk for more titles**

This book is dedicated to Kathryn Cheshire,
whose encouragement and understanding got me through
an incredibly difficult year. I simply could not have done
this book without your support and guidance.
You're awesome.

Also to my bestie, Marleine Dicks.
Thanks for all the reading you had to do of my earlier—
and really bad—manuscripts. I eventually got it right, but
I appreciate all the loving support and encouragement.
Thanks too for all the laughter you bring into my life.
I just wish we could spend more time laughing.

Praise for
Lucy Ryder

'*Resisting Her Rebel Hero* is an absolute delight to read…
the sexy writing and refreshing characters leave their mark
on every page.'

—*HarlequinJunkie*

CHAPTER ONE

"HEY, LADY! WATCH IT."

Dr. Holly Buchanan grimaced and threw a breathless "Sorry!" over her shoulder at the guy she'd nearly trampled as she dashed through the automatic doors into the huge marble lobby of West Manhattan Saints.

She was late. Late, late, *late*, damn it. And it was the second time this month. She should have suspected the morning would go to hell when she'd slept through her alarm and then broken the heel of her favorite designer pumps—hopping on one foot while trying to find the other shoe.

But nothing could have prepared her for the absolute chaos that greeted her when she'd opened her front door and found furniture and boxes piled up against her door, littering the stairs and sidewalk.

It had taken a few shocked moments to work out that the avalanche was meant for the neighboring brownstone and not hers. *Thank God.* Unfortunately, it had taken a lot longer to convince the mover—a scary tattooed guy who'd towered over her by at least a foot and a half—that the address he was looking for was right next door. *Not hers.*

He'd folded his huge tattooed arms across an even huger chest and stared at her with a level don't-even-think-of-messing-with-me-lady look that had made her quail in her strappy heels. And because he'd startled her, she'd blurted out the first thing that had come into her head: "Did you know that prison inmates in Russia use melted boot heels mixed with blood and urine to make tattoo ink?"

His answer, when it had come, had been accompanied by raised eyebrows and a wry twist of his lips. "Marine corps," he'd drawled in a voice that had seemed to come from his large booted feet. "One tattoo for every skirmish survived." And Holly had sucked in a mortified breath.

"Oh, my g-gosh, I'm s-sorry," she'd stammered, wanting the earth to open up and swallow her. "Th-thank you for your service."

He'd quirked an eyebrow and replied with a dry "You're welcome. Now, where should I put all this stuff?"

It had taken her time she hadn't had to convince him to call the moving company, which he did while guarding her door like a bouncer at a shady nightclub. After what had seemed like an age—during which Holly had bounced from foot to foot in extreme impatience—he'd finally apologized for the mistake. Then he'd reached over a box almost as tall as she was and gallantly lifted her as easily as if she were a child. To her shock he'd carried her down the box-littered steps and gently deposited her on the sidewalk with a cheerful "Wouldn't want you to twist an ankle in those shoes."

She'd mumbled a breathless "Thank you" and had risked more than a twisted ankle running for the subway.

Setting off across the huge lobby toward the bank of elevators, Holly dodged people heading in the same direction and tried to tell herself that elevators were mostly safe and that the hospital had a rigorous maintenance schedule.

She growled and skirted a crowd of nurses gathered around a large board the hospital used to announce upcoming events, lectures by visiting experts, and new staff appointments. She usually took an interest in any new announcements as she hoped her name would soon be featured when the plastic and reconstruction surgical fellowship was announced.

This morning, however, she barely gave it, or the oohing

and aahing women, a cursory glance as she streaked past, heels clicking on the slick marble floor. She hated being late for meetings with the chief of surgery. He wasn't exactly the kind of man you wanted to annoy—especially if you were a surgical resident hoping for that fellowship.

The doors of one lone elevator slid open with a ding and she sent up a quick prayer and dashed into the car just as a group of noisy teens emerged. As they shoved past, one sneakered foot caught Holly's ankle and sent her flying. She valiantly tried to halt her forward momentum by grabbing for the aluminum frame and forgot that she was carrying her briefcase. It went flying one way and she went the other, landing awkwardly on her hands and knees. She heard a muffled grunt and the next thing she knew the contents of her handbag and briefcase were exploding all over the floor.

The doors swished closed and there was a moment of stunned silence during which Holly thought, *You have got to be freaking kidding me!*

She sucked in air and snarled a few choice words that would turn her mother's hair gray. But, jeez, it had brought back memories she didn't like to think about. Memories of a wildly tilting elevator and frightened screams as it plummeted and then exploded on impact.

For a couple of beats she struggled with control before remembering having heard a grunt. She lifted her head, hoping Monday madness was giving her auditory hallucinations on top of everything else. The last thing she needed was someone having witnessed her graceless flight.

Please, let me be alone. Please, let me be alone.

Holly blew a few escaped strands of hair out of her eyes and froze when her vision cleared. Bare inches from her nose was a pair of large scuffed sneakers attached to the bottom of faded, soft-as-butter jeans. She blinked and followed the long length of denim up endless muscular legs to something that made her eyes widen and her mouth drop open. And before she could register that she was checking out some guy's impressive package, the man dropped to his haunches and Holly found herself staring into a pair of concerned blue-green eyes surrounded by a heavy fringe of sun-tipped lashes—on her hands and knees.

Sucking in a shocked breath, she wondered if she was more embarrassed by her position or the direction she'd been looking then promptly forgot everything when she felt the sensation of falling. Right into a swirl of gold-flecked blue and green. It was only when he opened his mouth and "You okay?" emerged in a voice as deep and dark as sin that she realized she'd been staring into his eyes as though she was submerged in the waters of the Caribbean and had forgotten how to breathe.

Her skin prickled and heated in premonition—of what, she wasn't entirely sure. But it felt like something monumental had just happened. Then, realizing what she was thinking, Holly gave a silent snort. *Yeah, right.* More like *monumentally* embarrassing.

His light eyes were startling in a tanned face that was both brain-ambushingly handsome and rugged. Like one of those naturally hot guys they used for advertising extreme sportswear. The kind of man who got his tan in the great outdoors—like standing on the prow of a pirate ship—and not from a tanning salon.

"Just peachy," she squeaked, swallowing her mortification at having sprawled at the feet of the hottest guy in Manhattan—maybe even America—and being caught eyeing his package then staring into his eyes like she'd been hypnotized.

Her belly quivered and for a second she wondered if the disrespectful little twerps had done her a favor. At least she now wouldn't have to suffer the additional indignity of swooning at his feet.

"You sure?"

"I'm f-fine," Holly croaked, her eyes dropping momentarily to his mouth, where the sight of well-sculpted lips tipped up in an almost-smile had her tongue swelling in her mouth like she was fifteen and crushing on a hot lifeguard. Her face flamed and she pushed back to sit on her heels. "Just incredibly embarrassed," she mumbled, brushing her hands together. "So, *please*…just ignore me and let me die with my dignity intact."

Crinkles appeared beside his amazing eyes and the corner of his mouth curled up even more, revealing—horror of horrors—a dimple. She caught herself staring at the shallow dent in his tanned cheek and gulped. *Darn*. He just had to have a dimple, didn't he? It was the one thing that could turn her into an awkward ninth-grader.

"I…er…" He cleared his throat and Holly looked up sharply, catching his attempts to suppress amusement. "I think it's a bit late for that."

She squeezed her eyes closed and gave a low moan of embarrassment. "G-great. Now I'm…." She sucked in a shaky breath and waved her hand in a quick dismissive gesture. "You know what, never mind."

Abruptly turning away, she looked around for her purse and briefcase. And there—in freaking plain sight for *everyone* to see—was her emergency stash of tampons, littering the floor like white bullets. And for just an instant she wished they were so she could just lock, load and pull the trigger to end her misery.

They reached for the closest tampon at the exact same moment and Holly squeaked, "I'll get that," quickly snatching it up and stuffing it into the bottom of her purse. She then pounced on the remaining cartridges, hoping he hadn't seen—but when she sent him a quick glance out of the corner of her eye and saw his teeth flash, she realized he had.

Oh, boy.

Pushing out her bottom lip, she huffed out a breath and lifted a wrist to shove aside tendrils of hair obscuring her vision. *Could her day get any worse?* Then a hand reached for hers and she forgot all about her crappy day when a snap of electricity bolted up her arm the instant their skins touched.

He too must have felt that audible little zap because he grunted softly and his eyes narrowed speculatively before he gingerly turned her hand over to inspect her scraped palm. She barely heard him rasp, "You're hurt," over the blood rushing through her ears.

The hand engulfing hers was large and tanned with long, surprisingly elegant fingers that drew her fascinated gaze even as they sent tingles rolling over her skin. Then his thumb was brushing gently over her scraped palm and the tingles became a raging firestorm of sensation that shot directly to her breasts and...well...further south.

Her eyes widened. *Oh...oh, wow.* What the heck was that? "It's n-nothing," she managed to croak, both to herself and him, before sliding her hand from his when she realized her mouth had dropped open and she was on the verge of babbling. She scooted back a little and sucked in a shaky breath, averting her face in the hope that he couldn't read her turmoil. Because, well...*darn.* The last time she'd been this flustered had been in the seventh grade when Jimmy Richards had caught her drawing hearts and flowers around his name.

Absently rubbing her tingling palm against her thigh, she stared at the jumble of her belongings and wondered what the heck she was supposed to be doing. It was only when she saw a half-eaten candy bar that she snapped to attention and began stuffing everything she could lay her hands on into her purse.

Holy cow. Where had all this stuff come from? She couldn't even remember having seen half of it before. Certainly not the gold pen or the roll of mints. And how many hairbrushes did one person need, anyway?

She left him to gather up her textbooks, study notes and stethoscope, thinking there was nothing in her briefcase that could embarrass her—until she remembered the old before-and-after photographs of herself that she kept as a reminder of why she was doing P&R.

Whipping around, Holly was relieved to see that the photos were nowhere in sight, but the guy was holding aloft a small foil square she hadn't even known she had. And if it *was* hers, it had to be at least two years old. Maybe even older.

Holly tried to look innocent, but it seemed the guy had an evil streak because he lifted a brow over gleaming blue-green eyes and drawled, "Medium?"

Oh, God, really? He was going to comment on the size?

"Keep it," she croaked. "Most condoms have a shelf life of four years, anyway. As long as you keep them in a cool, dry place." And nothing could be cooler or drier than the bottom of her briefcase, especially the past couple of years when she'd been focusing on the P&R fellowship and not relationships.

His grin turned wicked, deepening that dimple in his cheek. "Way too small," he said innocently, as though they were discussing a pair of shoes and not a freaking condom. He tilted his head and squinted at the printing on the back. "Besides, I think this one's already a year and a half past that four-year shelf-life date you were talking about."

Her face heated and she mentally rolled her eyes. *Way to let a hot guy know your sex life is non-existent, Holly.* She groaned silently and reached out with a growled "Just give it here," before tossing the package in the wall-mounted trash bin. For a couple of beats he stared at the stainless-steel receptacle then turned to her with a level look.

"You know someone is going to find that and use it, don't you?" He shook his head at her. "How do you think you'll feel knowing you had a hand—even unwittingly—in an unplanned pregnancy?"

"Ohmigod," Holly burst out, wondering if the torture of this day would ever end and what she'd done to deserve it. *"Fine!"* She opened the lid and fished it out, shudder-

ing when her fingers encountered something sticky. She shoved the errant condom into her pocket and glared at him challengingly. The unspoken words *Are you happy now?* vibrated in the air between them.

Eyes crinkling at the corners, he rose to his feet and offered her a hand but Holly ignored it and scrambled up—all embarrassing items finally hidden, thank God—before accepting her briefcase from him with a strangled mutter of thanks.

She was careful not to let their hands touch. Her body was buzzing with enough electricity to light up Manhattan for a day—and she hadn't even had her coffee yet.

Fortunately, the elevator dinged its arrival at her floor and when the doors opened she escaped, hoping she never saw him again. Just before the doors slid closed he called out a friendly "Don't forget to replace that condom, it's the responsible thing to do."

A few people heard and sent her curious looks but Holly ignored them, stomping down the passageway and muttering about *not* being responsible for her actions when it came to hot smartasses. It was only when she passed a startled nurse pushing a bassinet that she realized she was on the twentieth floor and not the twenty-second.

Muttering to herself, she changed direction and headed for the stairs, resigned to the fact that she was nearly fifteen minutes late for her meeting.

The moment she slipped into the boardroom she felt the eyes of every person in the room turn to watch her entrance, including the laser-blue stare of the chief of surgical residents, Professor Gareth Langley. Flushing, she ducked her head and murmured an apology, and slipped into the only open chair around the huge oval table.

Fortunately, with the day she was having, she wasn't scheduled for any surgery. She'd probably slice and dice her fingers—or worse.

Without looking up, she drew the nearest folder closer

and opened it, knowing she would find the new surgical schedule. There were other pages inside but Holly ignored them and quickly scanned the list, sighing her relief when she saw that she was scheduled for a number of procedures with Dr. Lin Syu and two with the head of plastic surgery, Dr. Geoff Hunt.

She lifted her lashes and caught Lin Syu's quick smile before she transferred her attention to the head of P&R, who was—*oh, joy*—looking right at her. She flushed beneath his questioning look and bit her lip but after a brief nod in her direction and a dry "Now that Dr. Buchanan has finally joined us…" Geoff Hunt turned away, shoving his hands into the pockets of his perfectly creased pants as he rocked back on his heels. "Perhaps we can get to the real reason Professor Langley is here this morning."

Now that the heat was off her, Holly let out a silent breath and relaxed into her chair, only half listening as Langley rose and began talking about the proposed expansion of the P&R department and the upcoming charity ball. It was a subject that he'd brought up before and one that Holly's mother—as CEO of Chrysalis Foundation—was involved in.

The Chrysalis Foundation worked solely for children and young people who needed plastic or reconstruction surgery but had no way of paying for the expensive procedures. It was also an organization her mother had started after Holly's own traumatic experiences.

Half listening, she let her gaze slide around the table but it came to an abrupt halt the instant she locked on a pair of amused blue-green eyes that were shockingly familiar. For the second time that morning—and it wasn't even nine a.m.—Holly felt the breath leave her lungs.

Her head went light, her stomach cramped and she thanked God she was sitting down because there in the chair next to Langley's was none other than…elevator guy.

Oh, God.

Her tongue emerged to moisten suddenly dry lips, and she wished she could grab the nearby water jug and drown herself before anyone noticed.

One eyebrow rose up his forehead and all Holly could think was... *Who the heck is he?*

Realizing she was staring at him all wide-eyed and open-mouthed, Holly jerked her gaze away to stare unseeingly at the columns of numbers on the screen, her mind racing with a kaleidoscope of images from the last half-hour. And when she realized she was absently rubbing her tingling palm down the length of her thigh she clenched both hands in her lap and struggled to control her breathing.

Maybe she'd dreamed up the entire episode. Maybe she was still asleep and dreaming.

Or having a nightmare, she snorted silently, and sneaked a peek at him. He was still watching her, his expression a mix of amusement and confusion—as though he didn't quite know what to make of her.

He wasn't the only one.

Frowning, she returned her unseeing gaze to Langley, nearly missing the part about the generous donation the hospital had recently received to expand P&R and finance the expensive new procedures they would be developing over the next five years, courtesy of a prominent Beverly Hills plastic surgeon.

It was the "Beverly Hills plastic surgeon" that caught Holly's attention and her gaze jerked back to elevator guy as a bad feeling landed in the pit of her stomach.

She sucked in a sharp breath at the wicked gleam lighting his changeable eyes and barely heard Langley's words over the blood thundering in her head.

Oh, God, please let me be wrong.

"I'm sure you all saw the announcement in the foyer this morning," Langley was saying, and elevator guy must have caught her stunned look because he gave a tiny shrug as though to say, You should have seen that one coming. But she hadn't. Not even close.

How could she have thought—even if she hadn't blown through the foyer—that the guy in the battered sneakers and well-washed jeans molded to every inch of his muscular thighs and well...*everywhere* was some big Hollywood celebrity cosmetic surgeon?

It's not him, Holly. It can't be.

Besides, where was the thousand-dollar suit, the eight-hundred-dollar, hand-stitched loafers and hundred-dollar haircut? She sneaked another peek at him and ran her gaze over all that tanned skin, sun-streaked hair and languid grace and decided she could see him gracing the cover of an extreme sports magazine—or maybe *Surf's Up*—more readily than a fancy Beverly Hills fundraiser.

But then Langley said, "I'd like to formally introduce Dr. Gabriel Alexander and welcome him to the West Manhattan family," and Holly realized with an unpleasant shock that the hot guy who'd made her knees wobble and her breath hitch in her chest was the very same man who'd been linked to rumors of new procedures and extreme body-sculpting of many Hollywood A-listers and supermodels. Including her famous sister.

What the heck was he doing in Manhattan?

He even had a dimple, *darn it!*

CHAPTER TWO

DR. GABRIEL ALEXANDER sighed and wedged himself into the movie-house-style chair, scooching down so he could tip his head back and finally close his eyes. It seemed like months instead of days since he'd shared a very interesting elevator ride with a certain surgical resident and he was exhausted—no thanks to said resident.

Crossing one ankle over the other on a backrest a few chairs down probably made him look like a long-legged spider squashed into a matchbox, but Gabe just needed some quiet time out from his hectic schedule. Besides, as a resident he'd slept anywhere; his favorite being observation rooms where it was usually quiet—especially after eight at night.

Popping his earphones in his ears, he sighed as rock music washed over him. It had only been four days since he'd been welcomed to West Manhattan Saints by a stunning briefcase-wielding assailant, but he kind of liked the vibe of being back in a large medical facility. Seems selling his partnership to some entitled young punk hungry for the Hollywood lifestyle had been the right decision after all.

For the past six years he'd been attached to a small private clinic that was so exclusive very few people even knew of its existence—except if you were famous, ultra-wealthy or both. Now, just thinking about what he'd left behind made Gabe shudder with an odd mix of pride, distaste and shame.

And if that didn't make him a candidate for the psych ward, nothing would. Not even his screwed-up childhood.

He'd had a mansion in Beverly Hills, a house in Santa Monica, a yacht and several luxury vehicles in his multiple-car garage and he'd been the most sought-after plastic surgeon on the West Coast. For a kid who'd spent his childhood believing he wasn't good enough, it had been a dream come true.

Looking back, he realized it had been a symbolic gesture to his rich and powerful grandfather. A man who'd used his connections to forcibly end the marriage of his son to a fellow student. A girl he'd deemed unworthy to carry the Alexander name—or the Alexander heir.

Only it had been too late for that. Third-year journalism student Rachel Parker had already been pregnant. When the old man had found out, he'd paid her a visit and along with thinly veiled threats told her to stay away from his family. Or else.

Afraid for her unborn child, Rachel had agreed. She'd moved across the country to ensure they never bumped into each other and Caspar Alexander had made sure that his son had been too busy—with his new wife and family— to be bothered with looking up his college flame. It hadn't stopped Rachel from telling her son all about his father and it hadn't stopped Gabe from dreaming—until he'd turned twelve—that his father would one day come to claim him. It had never happened. Both his father and his grandfather had conveniently gone back to their entitled lives as though nothing had happened.

Until about two years ago when the old man had decided he needed someone to take over the family business. It seemed Caspar's son and legitimate grandchildren were a huge disappointment and couldn't be trusted not to squander everything he'd spent a lifetime building.

The old man had told him how proud he was of Gabe's

achievements and that it was clear he was a chip off the old block.

Gabe had not so politely told him what he could do with his offer.

For a long time he'd been angry—at his mother and father—but especially the ruthless Caspar Alexander. And when he'd been invited to join the clinic he'd seen it as his ticket to the big league. *Look,* Gabe was saying to the old man. *I didn't need you or your family's money to become someone. I did it all by myself.*

Then his mom had been diagnosed with an aggressive form of leukemia and none of his money, contacts, fame or his skill with a scalpel had made a difference. By the time she'd slipped away, he'd realized his mother was right. He'd become the one thing he hated above all else. He'd become just like his grandfather. Ruthless, cold in his personal relationships and interested in only two things—money and status. It had been a rude awakening. One that had spurred him on to make some drastic changes in his life.

Someone bumped against the row of seats, jolting Gabe from the disturbing memories of his childhood and his nonexistent relationship with a man who'd pretended most of Gabe's life that he didn't exist.

Grateful for the disruption, he cracked open one eye to see that a small crowd had gathered at the observation window overlooking operating room three.

A quick look at the overhead OR screen gave him a close-up of an open torso and disembodied gloved hands wielding stainless-steel instruments with skill and precision. And considering that WMS had some of the best trauma surgeons on the east coast, whoever was on the table was in good hands.

Tugging on one earphone, he tuned into the murmur of voices around him and discovered that someone called Dr. Chang was working on a young woman who had landed beneath a bus during rush hour traffic.

He replaced the earphone and watched the onscreen action for a few more minutes, admiring the dexterity of the leading surgeon's hands, before letting his eyes drift over the observers.

They were painfully young and even if they hadn't been dressed in light blue scrubs, he would have pegged them as residents. Their fresh, animated faces reminded him of his own resident days, which meant they were probably not discussing whatever was going on below. Most likely it was about a hot nurse, or complaints about their supervisors.

Hospitals were like small towns where everyone knew everyone else and no one's personal business remained private for long. People gathered during quiet times to gossip about patients; nurses liked to complain about doctors and doctors liked to complain about everyone, especially Administration.

And Administration? Well, they were the common enemy because they hoarded funds like Scrooge, cutting costs and fighting every requisition from floor wax to MRI maintenance.

And, Gabe thought with a dry laugh, he hadn't even realized until now just how much he'd missed it. Not so much the gossip but he'd missed the camaraderie of a large medical facility where the haves and have-nots were locked in a daily battle of survival. It wasn't just a place where the rich and bored came to buy the latest style of face or body— or have a steamy affair with their attending surgeon. This was real.

Sighing, Gabe slid his gaze over the rest of the observation-room occupants before letting his eyes drift shut. He knew he should get up and return to his temporary digs, where a ton of boxes waited to be unpacked, but he just needed to—

Abruptly something he'd seen registered and his eyes snapped open to zero in on a familiar figure standing off to one side.

Dr. Holly Buchanan.

Mouth curving in appreciation, Gabe watched her focus on the overhead screen, her small white teeth nibbling on lush pink lips. A little frown of concentration marred the smooth skin of her forehead. Every so often her slender hands and long, elegant fingers would move in what he recognized was a replica of whatever was happening below— as though she was practicing or maybe committing the action to memory.

He'd spent enough time among the wealthy to recognize that Dr. Buchanan came from money, and lots of it. She even had that cool elegance that seemed to come naturally to the very wealthy. A cool elegance that sometimes hid an ugly belief that people they perceived as inferior were to be exploited and that their money and social status gave them that right.

He didn't have far to look for examples either. His own gene pool, for one. An old ex, for another. A girl he'd honestly thought had loved him enough to overlook the fact that he had been a half-starving med student from a very modest background.

But instead of standing up to her powerful family, she'd laughed at his declarations of love and told him she'd been using him to get back at her father—and have one final hot fling before she married a man eminently more suitable to their social circle.

Okay, so he'd been a young, foolish hothead, out to prove himself worthy. Prove that his story, at least, would have a happy ending. It had just proved to him that people born into wealth weren't interested in anything more than a hot fling with someone from the wrong side of town—especially someone they perceived as illegitimate.

But even though he knew Holly Buchanan was from a world whose vanity he'd happily exploited, he couldn't help watching her. Her appearance was as coolly classy as it had been the last time he'd seen her, scowling across the boardroom table as though he was personally responsible for the national debt.

But that's where the similarities ended. There was nothing cool about those large heavily fringed blue eyes. And knocked to her hands and knees, she'd muttered curses like someone tugging impatiently at the constraints of her upbringing.

Then there were those paper-thin scars that had been expertly covered with a light brush of foundation. Someone had either done a hatchet job on the stunning young surgeon or...or some horrific injuries had been expertly repaired. He wondered which it had been then decided it didn't matter considering both would explain her interest in plastic surgery.

But it was her eyes—or rather the unguarded expression in them—that had caught his attention. Despite that outer sophistication, Holly Buchanan, it seemed, wasn't as poised as she would like the world to believe, and he wondered what her story was.

He slid a hand to the bruise on his thigh where her briefcase had whacked him and spared a moment to be thankful that it hadn't connected higher. Any higher and he would have been on the floor, having an up-close-and-personal view of her tampons.

He chuckled, recalling the way she'd snatched them up and shoved them to the bottom of her purse as though they had been contraband and she'd been afraid he was the secret police. But then he'd found the condom packet and despite the wild color blooming in her cheeks, the ruffled kitten had flexed her tiny claws by insinuating he used a medium.

Gabe closed his eyes to the sight of her nibbling on her thumbnail and frowning at the overhead screen while she ignored the little upstart twerp trying to chat her up. There was something about her that struck a chord of familiarity but he was sure he'd never met or seen her before.

He was just drifting off when something made him open

his eyes to see her edging up the stairs, giving him a wide berth as though he was a slumbering tiger she didn't want to disturb. Suddenly several pagers began beeping and she froze mid-tiptoe, her eyes snapping toward him, widening in alarm when she caught him watching her.

The residents crowded up the stairs, elbowing each other and muttering curses about slave-driver supervisors as they bolted for the door. In the ensuing scuffle, Dr. Buchanan was roughly jostled aside and Gabe had a brief glimpse of one sexy heel catching on the stair runner. Her arms wind-milled in a frantic attempt at regaining her balance…and the next moment she was toppling onto Gabe with a muf-fled shriek.

His hands shot out to catch her but she landed with a startled "Oomph" right in Gabe's lap—and hard enough to have him seeing stars. When his vision cleared he had an armful of curvy, fragrant female squirming around like she was giving him a lap dance to end all lap dances. And because he was a red-blooded guy who hadn't been any-where near a woman in way too long, his body instantly reacted, waking up to the fact that a beautiful, sexy woman was butt-planted over his groin. He gave a low groan and she whipped around to gape at him like he'd zapped her with his shock stick.

Hey, not his fault. *Innocently minding my own business here, lady.*

One look into her mortified blue eyes and he realized that she was trying to get away and not turn him on but, damn…sue him, it had been a long time since he'd had *sex*, let alone been close enough to a woman to catch the heady scent of her skin.

Their gazes connected and she froze; her eyes wide on his. As though realizing her mouth was barely an inch from his, she gave a distressed bleat and tried again to free her-self, shoving at him at the same time as she tried to get her feet on the floor.

But the angle was wrong and the more she struggled, the more his eyes crossed and the more mortified she looked until he finally took pity on them both and rose to his feet in one swift move. She gasped at the abrupt change of elevation and clutched at him as though she anticipated being dumped on her ass.

It was probably that unflattering assumption that prompted his next action.

Instead of releasing her and stepping away like a gentleman would have, he kept one arm wrapped tightly around her waist and let her slowly slide down the full length of his body until her feet touched the floor.

He knew by the flicker of her lashes and the wild flush in her cheeks that she could feel more than the hard planes of his chest and thighs. The instant she got her feet under her, she sucked in air and shoved away from him, stumbling back a couple of steps. She would have fallen into the row of seats across the aisle if he hadn't shot out a hand and yanked her back.

Their bodies collided hard enough to momentarily knock the breath from his lungs and he wrapped an arm around her to keep her from flying off down the stairs. Okay, and maybe because he liked having all those soft curves pressed up against him.

"Careful," he murmured. "You don't want any more bruises to add to the ones you already have."

She froze and stared into his eyes, alarmed to find herself in the exact position she'd tried to escape from a couple seconds earlier.

"Who…who told you I have bruises?" she demanded in a breathless rush that made him wonder about things that he had no business thinking about. Like how she'd sound in the throes of passion. And where else she had a bruise that he could kiss better.

It was an entirely inappropriate thought—not to mention stupid given that his body clearly liked the visuals that popped fully formed into his head—to have about a younger colleague working toward a fellowship in the same department.

Realizing they were still plastered together like glue on paper, she made a sound of distress and eased out of his arms, this time careful not to make any sudden moves that might result in him having to save her.

She cleared her throat. "I mean, how do you know about the bruises?"

Gabe arched a brow and folded his arms across his chest, letting his gaze roam over the delicate creaminess of her face and neck. "You winced when you sat down at Monday's meeting and I'm guessing that creamy skin bruises easily."

She continued staring at him warily for a moment longer before she said, "Oh," as though she'd suspected him of following her into the ladies bathroom and spying on her as she'd checked out her smarting bottom and knees.

Gabe felt his mouth curve. He'd never met a woman whose every thought flashed across her face louder than Dr. Buchanan's. That they were hardly complimentary was an added bonus to a man who'd spent the last eight years of his life being wooed by women all wanting something from him.

"I'm sorry I disturbed your sleep," she said in that low, husky voice that seemed to reach out and stroke his flesh in places that hadn't been stroked in way too long. And when he lifted a brow she hastened to add, "And for...well, nearly flattening you."

"You hardly flattened me," he drawled. "Besides, I wasn't asleep, just resting my eyes. You learn a lot about people when they think you're comatose. Take the guy trying to get your attention." He could see she knew exactly who he was talking about when she bit her lip and looked away. "I overheard him bragging about his performance and wondered if he was talking about the OR, ER or someplace more private." Heat bloomed beneath her skin. "He's the kind of guy that gives surgeons a bad name."

Her eyes snapped to his and her face settled into a remote coolness that surprised him but not as much as her words. "The only surgeons who give us a bad name," she observed coolly, "are those arrogant enough to think they know better than God how to improve beauty."

Gabe was smart enough to know she was referring to him. He opened his mouth to defend himself but the anger and accusation filling her huge blue eyes stunned him into silence.

What the hell?

He wasn't to blame for her scars. Was he? He would certainly have remembered if she'd been a patient and there was no way he would have forgotten if he'd ever dated her—even briefly. Firstly, she wasn't his type and, secondly…well, secondly, he didn't think any man would be able to forget those big blue eyes or that lush wide mouth. Not in ten lifetimes.

Then he thought about her accusation and his anger died. She was right. For a long time he'd aggressively participated in the Hollywood pursuit of perfection until he'd reveled in the challenge of improving on Mother Nature's handiwork. A nip here, a tuck there and maybe even a complete body-sculpt to anyone who could afford it.

Thinking about it brought back the shame and disgust at the knowledge that he'd been as culpable as any one of his patients in their futile pursuit of perfection. But that didn't mean he was going to let her get away with her accusation—or her attitude, which, now that he came to think about it, had changed right about the time Langley had introduced him.

He shoved his hands in his pockets and rocked back on his heels. "Want to know what I learned about you?"

"No," she said quickly, and took a step toward him, only to stop abruptly when he didn't move aside because for some idiotic reason he didn't want to let her go. "I'm sure your insights are simply fascinating," she continued, frowning at her watch as though she was very busy and couldn't spare the time. "But I'm not that interesting."

Gabe smiled, because in the few days—encounters— that he'd known her, Holly Buchanan had been anything but uninteresting. He lifted a hand to scratch his jaw and paused, his eyes narrowing thoughtfully when she sucked in a tiny breath as though the rasp of beard-roughened skin was somehow too intimate in the quiet room.

"You're intensely focused, keep to yourself and practice with your hands without realizing it. You bite your thumb-nail when you're concentrating and hate being the center of attention. In fact, you mostly present only one side of your face to people you're talking to."

She bit her lip and looked away. Zeroing in on the move, he was suddenly tempted to lean forward and bite that plump lip too. But she was carrying her briefcase again and he didn't want to tempt her to use it as a weapon. This time her aim might just reach ground zero.

"How am I doing so far?"

He was rewarded when she rolled her eyes and pressed her lips together as though her silence would discourage him. He'd spent enough time strutting around California beaches during his adolescence to know when a woman was disinterested. He'd bet his entire surfboard collection that Holly Buchanan had been just as affected by their little skirmish as he had. Her dilated pupils, wild rosy flush and that soft gasp she'd given when she'd realized how close he was—and how hard—were as telling as the shiver that had gone through her.

She was attracted but determined to fight it. The question was why. What had he done to offend her?

"Okay," he mused, studying her through narrowed eyes. "My guess is you did all the girly-girl stuff, like ballet, piano and deportment. You probably feel like you have to excel at everything you do…maybe to make someone happy. Mother? Father? Boyfriend?" Her mouth dropped open and he grunted with displeasure at the notion. "Is it a boyfriend?"

"As if!" she practically squawked, and he smirked, strangely pleased by her reaction. Seeming embarrassed by her outburst, Holly pressed her lips together and tried to look bored.

He scratched his jaw again before sliding his gaze over her face, touching briefly on those silvery white scars. "I'd say your interest in plastic surgery stems from your own experiences or maybe some deep-seated need to fix other people's mistakes."

Her hand rose swiftly and then froze in mid-air, as though she was fighting an instinctive reaction to hide her face, and Gabe felt his gut clench as though he'd been carelessly insensitive.

Fighting the urge to wrap his arms around her and pull her into the safety of his arms—which was shocking enough—he let his gaze slide over her classically classy outfit, lingering overly long on her breasts, covered but not hidden by the expert fit of her jacket. He suddenly knew exactly how to put that spark of rebellion in her eyes and get the stubborn tilt back to that Irish chin.

"Or maybe I've got it completely wrong," he drawled smoothly, making no secret of the direction of his gaze. "Maybe I'm not the only one into cosmetic surgery?"

For a moment she stared at him like he'd uttered an obscenity before she huffed out a breath and crossed her arms beneath her breasts, making Gabe wonder if it was to hide from his gaze or keep from taking a swing at him.

"That's just insulting," she snapped, and Gabe grinned. He kind of liked the idea that she was struggling with some pretty intense feelings and he didn't mind the idea of getting into a tussle with her if she did take a swing at him.

In fact, he would enjoy it. Probably more than he should.

He expected a scathing response—or maybe a request

for him to get the hell out of her way. What he didn't expect was for her to open her mouth and say, "Did you know that women with breast implants are three times more likely to commit suicide or develop drug- and alcohol-related dependencies?"

Gabe tore his attention from her breasts with a "Huh?" and wondered if he'd heard correctly. She flushed and sucked in air before continuing and he struggled to connect the random facts with what they'd been discussing.

"Two-thirds are repeat clients."

"O-o-okay...." Well, he could certainly attest to that fact. But what the hell did that have to do with—?

"In fact," she continued peevishly, as though she held him personally responsible for women's dissatisfaction with their bodies, "more than five million Americans are addicted to plastic surgery, spending about thirteen billion dollars annually on a variety of procedures. That's enough to rival the national debt of a small country."

She stared at him as though waiting for his response but he wasn't sure what he would say if he did. Instead, he studied her silently for a couple of beats, his mouth slowly curling up at one corner. "Uh-huh. That's quite fascinating but doesn't really answer my question."

She rolled her eyes and muttered something that sounded like "Never mind," before taking a bold step toward him, no doubt hoping good manners would prompt him to move out of her way.

"I have mace," she announced when he remained blocking her escape.

"No, you don't," he disputed, his grin growing into a chuckle when she blew out a frustrated breath. Her eyes narrowed to dangerous slits and her hand tightened on her briefcase as though she contemplated whacking him with it. "I know exactly what you have in there, remember," he said, angling his shoulders just enough for her to slip past but not enough that she could avoid touching him.

But Holly Buchanan was obviously no pushover because just before she stomped from the room she sent him a level stare all women seemed to develop in the womb that said he was lower than slime for behaving like a jerk.

But, really, he didn't know of one guy who wouldn't have.

For a long moment he admired the straight spine, slender, curvy hips twitching with annoyance as she headed down the passage. The strappy heels that had caused at least one of her accidents this week tapped out an irritated beat on the tiled floor that for some odd reason he found damn sexy.

"By the way," he called out, "did you know that the world's largest condom is two hundred and sixty feet long with a base circumference of three hundred and sixty feet?" And when she paused in her stride and sent him a *what-the-heck?* look over her shoulder, he shrugged. "I'm just saying. Mediums are only good as water bombs."

CHAPTER THREE

HOLLY ROLLED HER eyes and set off down the passage at a fast clip, muttering to herself about men never growing up. While it was mostly true and not worth losing sleep over, it certainly beat thinking about her humiliating tumble into the lap of the one man she wanted to avoid. Or his physical reaction to her squirming around on his lap like a second-rate stripper hoping for a big tip.

Her face burned. *And, boy, had she been given the biggest tip of her life.* Before she could stop it, her skin prickled and heated and her heart set off like a vampire bat scenting warm blood. *Oh, God.* And to think that humiliating little incident had actually turned her on. Maybe this all-work-and-no-play plan of hers was making her a little crazy. Maybe all she needed was a few hours of hot, sweaty, heart-pumping exercise—at the gym, she added hastily—and she could get back to focusing on her plan to get the fellowship.

Besides, she was so close that she couldn't let herself get distracted. Not now and certainly not by a guy who either nipped and tucked women into physical perfection or made the backs of their knees sweat.

Groaning inwardly, Holly increased her pace, as though she could outrun the memory of hard thigh and belly muscles pressed firmly against her bottom and then from chest to knee—and *everything* between—as she'd slid down the front of his hard frame.

She got a full-body tingle just thinking about it. A gasp of horror burst out. Full-body tingle? *Oh, God.*

Absolutely no freaking way. And not with him.

Focus on the plan, Buchanan, and *not* on the way he makes your knees wobble or the fact that medium was too small. No. Not too small, she corrected a little hysterically. *Waa-aay* too small.

Oh, boy. And since she'd inadvertently stared at his package, she would probably agree. She got another full-body shiver and muttered a curse when it slid down her spine like a delicious thrill.

Stop that, Holly, she ordered sternly, *he's the guy that turned Paige's respectable B-cups into C pods.* And for what? So he could make a few thousand bucks? So her sister could flash a bigger cleavage to all her adoring "fans" when she appeared on the latest magazine cover? Or went topless on Bimini?

Big deal. Especially when there were people out there scarred by life-altering events who didn't have access to even basic medical care, let alone cutting-edge plastic surgery.

Weren't there enough butchers willing to slice and dice in the name of vanity that West Manhattan could focus on building the best P&R center in the world? Besides, everyone knew that most women would never be satisfied with their looks, no matter what.

She was trying so hard to convince herself that there were no redeeming qualities about Dr. Hotshot from Beverly Hills that she failed to realize the man himself had caught up with her until a flash of movement drew her attention.

Her stride wobbled for an instant but she sucked in a fortifying breath and marched on, determined to ignore him. Besides, she needed all her concentration to keep upright or she might end up breaking something the next time she took a tumble.

She grimaced. She'd seen him a total of three times and

managed to embarrass herself each time. Despite her klutzy childhood, it was probably a new record.

She clenched her jaw and sent him a narrow-eyed look out the corner of her eye but he appeared oblivious to her presence, loping along beside her with an easy, loose-limbed stride that was deceptively indolent, as though he was alone and liked it that way.

Holly rolled her eyes and ignored the pinch in her chest. *Yep, story of my life.* The hot guys always ignored her—especially when they discovered she wasn't perfect, like the rest of her family. That she wasn't as outgoing as her famous sister or as warm and beautiful as her mother.

Not that she *wanted* him to notice her, she amended quickly, especially if it meant she didn't have to make conversation.

"Are you following me?" she asked coolly, rolling her eyes at the faint huskiness in her voice.

So much for not wanting conversation.

He turned his head and their eyes met for a couple of beats until Holly felt the soles of her feet tingle. "I'm headed home," he said mildly. "Although…I could probably be talked into dinner somewhere dark and smoky."

She caught his harmlessly hopeful smile, which did absolutely nothing to reassure her—especially when his eyes gleamed all wickedly amused and challenging. But it was the smoldering heat in them that stole all her bones right along with her breath and common sense.

Gabriel Alexander was about as harmless as a tiger in a supermarket and had most likely perfected the art of seduction before he could walk.

"No? Coffee, then?" he suggested in that deep hypnotic voice that invited women to do things they wouldn't normally do. Things *she* wouldn't normally do, but was suddenly tempted to try. "Besides being starving, I thought I might be useful."

Useful? Holly licked her lips. Completely against her

wishes, her thoughts turned recklessly to just how useful he could be—to her exercise plan, of course—and then wondered if she was advertising her thoughts like a neon sign in the desert when his teeth flashed white in his handsome, tanned face. And because the notion flustered her, she blurted out, "Did you know that silicone is a better choice than rubber for medical purposes because it is more heat- and UV-resistant?"

Realizing what she'd said, she squeezed her eyes shut and prayed for death. *Ohmigod.* Wouldn't it be easier to just walk into the nearest wall? Or maybe step out into traffic? Because clearly the man just had to look at her and her mouth disconnected from her brain.

"It's also better at resisting chemical and fungal attacks, which makes it more durable," she finished miserably and when he made a noise that sounded suspiciously like a chuckle she glared at him, only to find him looking back at her with polite interest—as if blurting out random stuff was normal.

"Now, that I do know," he revealed, hitching a shoulder in a smooth, boneless move that she envied. "I spent most of the eighth grade water-bombing the girls' locker room. The fact that latex is so flexible means it's more prone to breaking when stretched beyond its limits." His teeth flashed. "But don't worry, you're safe. I've grown out of the urge to hear girls scream at the sight of latex."

Yeah, right, Holly thought a little hysterically. *Safe, my eye. He was probably* still *making women scream—before wreaking havoc with their hearts.*

And when she felt queasy at the thought of him making some faceless woman scream, she turned away from his appealing smile before she gave in to the urge to return it—or maybe smack him for making her forget her plan.

Just then the automatic doors opened to reveal a uniformed porter and Holly could have kissed the older man in sheer relief.

On seeing her, the porter's face broke into a wide, craggy smile. "Evening, Doc," he greeted her in his heavy Brooklyn accent. "No big date tonight?" Holly shook her head as she did every time he asked and he clicked his tongue, sending the man beside her a reproving look. "It's a sad day when a beautiful girl doesn't have someone to wine and dine her at one of those fancy downtown restaurants. What is the world coming to?"

Dr. Alexander sent her a silent look and shrugged as if to say, *I did offer.* Narrowing her eyes, Holly was seriously tempted to lie. Besides, she did have a date. Sort of. That it was probably takeout from the pizza place around the corner from the brownstone she shared with a couple of other surgical residents, along with a bottle of wine and a gallon of ice cream, was beside the point. A date was a date.

Conscious of blue-green eyes watching her, Holly flushed. "Dating isn't in my plan," she told the older man. "At least, not right now," she hastened to add when a soft snort reached her, and she wished she carried a stun gun in her purse because he now also knew that she didn't date. And found it amusing. *The jerk.*

"Plans change, Doc. Besides, you're not getting any younger," the porter advised, and Holly ground her back teeth together when Dr. Hollywood's snort turned into a cough. "Want me to call you a cab?"

"I'm fine, thank you."

She was tempted to add that she wasn't entirely opposed to dating. Just not right now, thank you very much. Besides, the last guy she'd been serious about had taken one look at her sister Paige and decided perfection was better for his image than scarred and brainy.

That Holly had thought to surprise Terrence Westfield one night and had found Paige already there—in his bed—was beside the point. The two of them had been discussing Holly like she was a freak and laughing about how naive she was to think a handsome guy like him could be inter-

ested in her. It had been even more devastating to discover
that Terrence had only dated her to get her father's attention in the hope that he could get an internship at her father's law firm.

She could have told him that Harris Buchanan only had
time for his son and couldn't care less whom she dated.

When—*if*—she found a man who was either blind or
could look beyond the surface flaws to the woman deep inside, she might risk it, but she first wanted to prove to herself
that she didn't need to be perfect or beautiful to succeed.

Sighing, she turned to see Dr. I-Can-Make-Women-
Scream watching her silently.

"What?"

His mouth turned up at the corners but his gaze was
unreadable.

"Wanna share a cab?"

Holly quickly shook her head. She was suddenly eager
to get away from him before she made a bigger fool of herself—which would be difficult after…well, everything that
had happened.

"No. Thank you."

He studied her silently for a couple of beats until head-
lights lit them up like they were on Broadway, signaling
the cue for them to launch into a heart-rending duet. But
this wasn't a Broadway musical and she couldn't carry a
tune to save her life.

He casually lifted his arm like a born-and-bred New
Yorker and like magic the empty cab slid to a stop. Holly
ground her teeth together. She usually had to step into traffic and risk serious injury before a cabbie deigned to stop.
And then it was mostly to yell abuse at her for being a "crazy
chick with a death wish."

"You sure?"

She swallowed an odd sensation that felt very much like
disappointment—but couldn't possibly be—at his immi-

nent departure, and nodded before she changed her mind.
"I'm sure."

After a moment he shrugged. "Suit yourself." And leaning forward, he opened the cab door. Half expecting him
to move aside so she could get in, Holly was momentarily
distracted when he propped his arm on the top of the door
and looked back at her, eyes dark and unreadable.

"See ya, Doc," he said, and slid into the cab, leaving
Holly to gape at the departing vehicle.

Chivalry, it seemed, even California celebrity style, was
well and truly dead.

The following week Holly had nearly double the number of
scheduled procedures and didn't have a lot of time to brood.
Her life was right on track with the plan and her goal was
within sight. There wasn't time—or the inclination, she reminded herself—to be thinking about wicked blue-green
eyes, let alone getting the opportunity to scream.

But that was easier said than done, especially when she
happened to look up during a breast reduction plasty to
see a familiar figure in the observation room. Only this
time he wasn't sprawled bonelessly across the seats, head
tipped back and eyes closed as his headphones pumped
music into his ears.

With his long legs planted wide and his folded arms test-
ing the seams of his black T-shirt, he looked like a modern-
day pirate on the deck of his ship as he challenged the sea.
And although his expression and his eyes were in shadow,
Holly knew he was looking right at her.

She could feel the weight of that cool, assessing gaze
and froze in familiar panic. It was only for an instant and
scarcely noticeable by the people around her, but it sent her
pulse racing and made her thighs tingle.

"Dr. Buchanan?" The calm voice of Lin Syu made her
blink and suck in a fortifying breath. She dropped her gaze

briefly to the attending surgeon, who was waiting for Holly's next move with a raised dark brow.

Altering her grip on the miniature scalpel, Holly prepared to make the inverted T incision that would both lift and reduce the size of the breast once the excess tissue had been removed.

She carefully followed the guidelines already drawn onto the skin. The patient, a thirty-four triple-D, with back, neck and shoulder problems, couldn't join her sports-crazy fiancé in outdoor pursuits because her heavy breasts caused discomfort, chronic pain and embarrassment. Kerry Gilmore had admitted that she'd spent her entire high-school years hiding her body and being unable to do things other girls did. Normal things like horseriding, swimming or joining the cheerleading squad. But it was the chronic pain that had finally made the decision for her.

She wanted her life back and Holly was preparing to do just that.

Exchanging the scalpel for surgical scissors, Holly carefully began separating the sectioned dermis from the breast tissue. The aim was to maintain a healthy blood supply to the nipple or it would turn necrotic. The drawback to any reduction was that large amounts of tissue were fed by a lot of blood vessels. Each time she nicked one of them, she waited while the OR nurse cauterized it and mopped up the blood.

Once the dermis had been properly detached from the breast tissue, Holly transferred it into the waiting hands of the attending nurse and went to work on excising the glandular and adipose tissue as per Lin Syu's murmured instructions.

By the time they'd removed five hundred grams of tissue from each breast, Holly was ready for the next stage. She and Dr. Syu made several complicated knots around the areola before gently lifting the nipple into its new position and nudging the remaining parenchyma into place.

She then temporarily closed and stapled the skin flaps so

she could assess the size, shape and position of each breast. The specialized operating table lifted the patient into a sitting position while Holly used the sizer to check the positioning before gently removing the staples and peeling back the skin flaps.

She attached strips of acellular mesh to the upper breast substance to strengthen the weakened muscles then patiently reconnected the mass to the dermal layers using a resorbable intradermal suture. This would reduce the pull of gravity and wound tension, speeding up recovery. It would also help keep scarring to a minimum.

She sutured the areola to the surrounding flaps before reaching for the staple gun for the final stage of the dermal resectioning procedure. When it was over she stepped back to allow the nurse to swab the wound sites with iodine in preparation for the daisy strips that would be applied around the areola in widening circles. They would serve a double function of protecting the wound from infection as well as provide additional support while the patient healed.

Five hours after the patient went under; Lin Syu supervised the insertion of the twin drains while Holly stripped off her mask, gloves and headgear.

"Excellent work, Dr. Buchanan," the older woman said, finally lifting twinkling black eyes to Holly. "We'll have you doing all our cosmetic procedures before long."

Holly grimaced, as Dr. Syu had known she would, and moved away from the table—her part of the procedure currently over. She sent a quick look up to the observation-room window and wasn't surprised to find it empty. Breast reductions weren't that interesting unless you were considering specializing in plastic surgery. And since Dr. Hot Celebrity was rumored to have done hundreds if not thousands of boob jobs, he had probably only wanted to rattle her.

And succeeded. *Darn it.*

"As long as the patient is satisfied with her new size," she said, stretching out cramped back and shoulder muscles as she moved toward the doors. She knew that she would have to perform cosmetic procedures but in this case it helped knowing she could restore someone's self-confidence while alleviating their pain.

Dr. Syu followed, stripping off her gloves. "You just saved her from a lifetime of pain and discomfort, Holly. That she wants to wear a bikini on her honeymoon doesn't make cosmetic procedures wrong."

Holly stifled a yawn. "I know," she mumbled, feeling somewhat chastened. "Besides being the object of curiosity and ridicule, Kerry Gilmore said she was tired of men making lewd comments about her breasts."

"Well, that's just juvenile and typical," Lin said in disgust. "Anyway, as long as she follows medical advice and wears the support garment, she'll be wearing her string bikini on her honeymoon come summer."

She untied Holly's surgical gown and waited while Holly returned the favor before saying over her shoulder, "You don't have to like them but you also shouldn't forget that cosmetics procedures—especially the big-bucks ones—help fund the reconstructions."

Holly sighed. Dr. Syu was right. Besides, she had firsthand experience of the emotional trauma caused by others' perceptions to be reminded of why she'd chosen to specialize in plastic and reconstruction surgery.

She'd spent her entire childhood struggling against the stereotype of beauty-versus-brains and was tired of people judging her by her looks or her family's accomplishments.

As a child she'd often thought she'd been adopted, switched at birth or maybe dumped on their doorstep by a wicked witch. It was only much later that she had accepted she was dark like her father and brother. At the time, though, she'd felt like an alien—a thin, scrawny, ugly duckling that her father couldn't possibly love.

She'd been clumsy, awkward and—she'd be the first to admit—cripplingly shy, geeky and snotty as hell. She'd hated being compared to her incredibly beautiful, blonde outgoing mother and her famous photographic model sister. And because she couldn't compete with her brother or sister for their father's attention, she'd tried to be the smartest so he could be proud of her too. And just when she'd begun filling out and growing into her large eyes, big mouth and long legs, she'd fallen a couple of stories when the cable on a glass elevator had snapped.

She'd been forced to undergo countless surgeries to repair the damage caused by flying glass, once again becoming the object of ridicule and pity. Boys who hadn't known about her accident had even called her The Scar, like she was some kind of comic-book villain or something.

"So," Lin Syu said casually, jolting Holly out of disturbing memories of her past. "What do you think of the new guy?"

Holly froze. "The new guy?"

"Yep." Dr. Syu dropped her soiled surgical gown into the hamper. "Our new celebrity hunk. I hear the nurses are all fighting to get on the surgical roster with him."

Holly rolled her eyes as heat crept up her neck. "I really hadn't noticed." Lin eyed her levelly, expression wry as though she could see right through Holly's lie. "What?" Holly asked, trying to look innocent. "I've been busy."

"So the looks that day at the meeting were my imagination?"

"What looks?"

"Everyone paying attention saw the looks, Dr. Buchanan." She grinned and waggled her eyebrows. "I just wondered if you two already knew each other or if it was lust at first sight."

Holly's head shot up, eyes wide with shock. "*Wha-at? I don't… Ohmigod!*" she spluttered, feeling her face burn with mortification as she thought back to those oddly intimate moments in the elevator and then again when their eyes had met across the boardroom. She hadn't thought anyone had seen. Clearly she hadn't been as discreet as she'd thought.

Her body instantly reacted to the memory of that weird sensation of the earth wobbling off its axis and she shivered and huffed out a breath.

"That's…um…" She gulped and cast around for something intelligent to say but all that emerged from her mouth was a strangled gurgling sound that Dr. Syu seemed to find hilarious.

Struggling to get her emotions under control and stall for time, Holly busied herself by carefully folding her soiled surgical gown and placing it neatly in the hamper.

"It's n-not what you think," she finally murmured, huffing out a couple of breaths like she was about to give birth. "But we…um, did meet in the elevator on the way up."

The surgeon pulled off her mask and cap and waited patiently for Holly to elaborate. When she didn't, Lin's brows rose up her forehead. "That must have been some meeting," she drawled, snorting out a laugh when Holly uttered a sound of distress. "I think he likes you."

Holly averted her head and wished she could sink through the floor. "That's…that's ridiculous," she denied a little too hastily. "Guys like him aren't…well…interested in people like um…" She gestured vaguely to her face. "Like me."

"You're a beautiful—yes, Holly," Lin insisted when Holly opened her mouth to argue, "beautiful and graceful woman. Not to mention a skilled and talented surgeon. Why wouldn't he be interested? He's a man, isn't he?"

"I wasn't always graceful," Holly admitted dryly, recalling how elegant she must have looked on her hands and knees. "It took a lot of hard work on my mother's part. Even now when I'm flustered…I, um…" She broke off, flushing when she realized what she was about to reveal.

"You what?

Holly sighed. "My…inner klutz emerges," she mumbled,

then grimaced when Lin snorted. "It's like I'm fifteen again and have no control over my feet or my mouth."

"And he flusters you? Hmm." Lin's mouth curved and her eyes twinkled with wicked humor. "I sense a story there," she said, just as her pager went off. "Which will unfortunately have to wait. Damn. Just when I thought I could finally get to know my kids again. They probably think I'm just the woman that comes in at night to sleep with their father before disappearing again in the morning." She sighed and threw "Great job in there, by the way," over her shoulder as she hurried off.

Holly took a moment to savor the senior surgeon's praise and went off in the direction of the locker rooms to change before heading home. She knew she should go to her office and catch up on paperwork but she'd promised her housemates that she'd be home for dinner.

It had been kind of weird since Kimberlyn Davis had moved in after her cousin Caren had left and then Tessa Camara, another surgical resident at WMS, had moved out, leaving Holly in a house of strangers. Okay, Sam Napier wasn't exactly a stranger but, then, the hot brooding Scot wasn't all that easy to get to know.

He mostly kept to himself but in a house filled with women she couldn't really blame him. She'd kind of had a little crush on him when he'd first moved in but he was a bit intimidating and didn't share himself with others. Thanks to her scars and her incredibly geeky adolescence, she still felt shy and awkward around him.

Tessa, who'd basically moved in with her fiancé, Clay, since she'd dropped the baby bombshell a couple months ago, had promised to join them for dinner. After the week Holly had had she was ready to talk about babies and forget about big bad celebrity doctors who could make women scream.

CHAPTER FOUR

GABE SLID INTO the back of a cab and gave the cabbie his Brooklyn address as he sank back against the seat. He'd been invited to join a few colleagues at a nearby bar but he'd been on call for over two weeks straight and he was exhausted. Besides, he still hadn't finished unpacking his boxes and he was sick of living out of suitcases and eating out of cardboard cartons.

He wanted real food that he'd cooked himself and he hadn't even had time to unpack his kitchen stuff.

When he couldn't swim or surf, cooking relaxed him. He didn't know if it was growing up in California, where everyone was a health nut or alternative lifestyle guru, but he liked eating freshly prepared food.

What he hated was eating alone. But that was something that couldn't be helped, especially after the telephone conversation he'd had earlier that day with his grandfather. Talking—if the cold, stilted exchange could be termed talking—with the old man always left him restless and angry.

He wondered how the old man had found out he was in New York then decided he didn't want to know. The less he knew about Caspar Alexander's business, the better. Besides, the only thing he had in common with his grandfather—or with his father, for that matter—was their last name and a few bad genes. Everything else he'd got was from his mom. *Thank God.*

The cabbie turned a corner and hooted at some poor pedestrian who'd had the bad judgment to cross at a green light, jolting Gabe out of his disturbing thoughts. This was a new chapter in his life and he didn't intend to ruin it by thinking about the sharks in his paternal gene pool. That was about as productive as standing in an observation room, watching a woman do a breast reduction plasty when he had rounds and a ton of paperwork waiting.

He may have been watching the skilled movements of Holly Buchanan's hands but he'd been thinking about those long, slender fingers on his skin. And when he'd realized that he'd been getting turned on, he'd left before someone in the OR had looked up and noticed his jeans had been a tight fit.

The cabbie pulled up in front of a neatly refurbished brownstone and Gabe got out, bending to glare at the guy through the open passenger window when he called out an outrageous fare.

The cabbie shrugged. "I have a wife and three daughters," he explained, accepting the notes shoved at him.

"My condolences," Gabe drawled, slapping a hand on the yellow roof as the cab roared off. He swore he heard the guy laugh and call him a crazy dumbass before the taillights disappeared around the corner.

Turning to survey the building he was temporarily calling home, he wondered if he'd made the biggest mistake of his life to have replaced his Santa Monica home with its sunny view of the ocean for this.

Sighing wearily, he shoved a hand through his rumpled hair and headed across the sidewalk. All those boxes waiting to ambush him weren't going to unpack themselves and he was tired of dodging obstacles and stubbing his toes.

Even before he'd received the phone call from West Manhattan, inviting him to join the P&R department, he'd been questioning the direction his life had taken. And thinking about that direction made him think about his mother, and his heart squeezed.

"Apparently you raised a crazy dumbass, Mom," he muttered, rubbing the heel of his hand over the pinch of grief in his chest. And then in the next instant he gave a rueful smile as he imagined how she'd react. She'd level her green gaze at him and say that it was better to be a crazy dumbass than a capitalist warlord—which was what she'd called his grandfather. His father, on the other hand, had the dubious honor of being the warlord's sidekick.

His mouth twisted in a bitter-sweet smile. *Damn* but he missed her. He missed her oddball sense of humor and the absolute joy she'd found in simple things; like growing herbs and making her own dandelion wine or chamomile tea, or scavenging wild herbs for her colorful salads. As a kid he'd been embarrassed by the weird stuff she'd made him eat and recalled how the other kids had used to torment him for being too poor to afford real food.

They hadn't been that poor and she hadn't tolerated any rudeness—from him or his friends. Her narrow-eyed stare had often been used to make him question some of his decisions. Like getting caught on camera, tp'ing the principal's car or being forced to clean the girls' bathroom after bombing it with paint-filled balloons.

He wondered what she'd have said about Holly Buchanan, blurting out random facts one minute, falling at his feet or into his lap the next, only to have her duck through the closest doorway to avoid him the rest of the time.

She'd probably laugh, say it served him right for being so pretty and then she'd tell him to hold onto the girl because she was obviously smart and he needed someone who wouldn't be taken in by his I'm-up-to-no-good smile.

But Gabe didn't need to hold onto anyone, especially a woman like Holly Buchanan. He'd fallen hard for a girl from her world once and had learned the hard way that they didn't consider guys like him suitable for anything but a good time. He'd been happy to comply ever since, keeping his relationships superficial and short-lived.

He'd never told anyone about his father out of respect for his mother. She was gone now but he no longer had any interest in people knowing that the owner and CEO of the company holding the largest US government defense contract was his grandfather, a man who'd told Gabe's pregnant mother to "get rid of it" because "it" wasn't good enough for the Alexander name.

Holly Buchanan might look at him like he was a decadent dessert and she was looking to fall off the diet wagon, but she'd made it perfectly clear that he wasn't part of her plan. No doubt she also had some eligible socially acceptable fiancé tucked away somewhere until she could fit marriage into her plan.

Besides not wanting to go down that path again, Holly was a colleague and Gabe didn't date colleagues—especially the young vulnerable ones depending on his professionalism for their career advancement.

He was heading for the stairs to his front door when he heard the sound of an approaching vehicle and turned just as a bright yellow cab pulled up beneath the streetlight. Even before the vehicle came to a stop, the passenger door opened and a strappy black sandal emerged.

Curious, he angled his head to get a better view and caught sight of a pale slender foot attached to the strappy feminine contraption. And when the sight set his heart pounding and his grip tightening on his house keys, he froze, because...because it was suddenly the most erotic sight in the world.

What the—?

Where the hell had that thought come from? Especially as he'd never had a fetish for women's footwear before. It either meant he needed sleep or had lost what was left of his mind. Considering he'd sold a hugely lucrative practice back in LA to join the staff of a Manhattan teaching hospital, it was most likely the latter.

His fascinated gaze took in the endless length of perfectly creased trousers and the slender curvy form that followed. He let out a soundless whistle when he recognized it as one he'd had plenty of opportunity to study over the past couple of weeks—usually disappearing through the nearest doorway to avoid him.

Oblivious to his scrutiny, she tugged briefly at the neat little black jacket and bumped the door closed with her hip while rummaging around in her shoulder bag.

She bent at the waist—giving Gabe an eyeful of her long slender legs and perfectly rounded bottom—and thrust her arm through the open passenger window. She said something to the cabbie that had him gesticulating wildly and Gabe decided she was probably cursing the hefty fare.

She turned with a muttered "Darn highway robbery," and stumbled back a step when Gabe chuckled in sympathy. Her sharply indrawn breath was clearly audible on the quiet street.

"Hey, careful," he called out before he could help himself, and breathed a sigh of relief when she didn't go ass over head into the street.

"*Ohmigosh*, D-Dr. Alexander, you scared me," she squeaked, and cast a nervous glance at the departing cabbie as though she was considering running after it. "Um… are you…are you coming to dinner?"

She cast a surreptitious look between him and the neighboring front door as though she was considering making a mad dash for it and suddenly all Gabe's moodiness and grief vanished and he found himself smiling.

Propping his shoulder casually against a huge earthenware pot halfway up the stairs, he studied her in the pool of light cast by the old-fashioned streetlamp.

Was the lady surgeon a neighbor or visiting? he mused. Or living with her husband or I—?

For some reason the idea of her with a lover annoyed him and then he wondered why the hell he cared. He didn't. Besides, she was exactly the kind of woman he'd promised he would never get involved with—the kind that fitted perfectly into his grandfather's world. Rich, classy and uptight.

He arched a brow. "Are you inviting me to dinner, Dr. Buchanan?"

A hunted look came into her eyes. "What? No…I mean… I thought that's why you're here." She sucked in an audible breath. "Aren't you?"

Gabe watched the conflicting emotions flash across her mobile features. After a couple of beats he took pity on her and held up his keys.

"Relax, Doc," he drawled, wondering why the idea of her going to dinner with some faceless man made his teeth ache. "These are my new digs."

She looked stunned and more than a little disturbed by the news as she edged up the neighboring stairs. "Your new, um…digs?"

"Uh-huh." He looked at her sideways and tried not to laugh at the sight of her nibbling on her thumbnail. It was something he'd noticed she did when she was disturbed. "Why, did you think I was stalking you again?"

"Wha—? No!" She gave an embarrassed laugh that ended on a cough. "Why would I think that?"

"I don't know," he said mildly. "Maybe because you're usually using escape-and-evade tactics that would do a marine proud."

"That's…that's just ridiculous," she spluttered, and even in the ambient light Gabe saw the guilty flush rise up her neck into her face. "We work on the same floor and…" She shrugged helplessly. "It's been hectic."

"Uh-huh." He folded his arms across his chest. "Would it help if I told you that you're not really my type?" He knew he'd thought it before but he'd been wrong. *She was so his type.* He shook his head and laughed again. This time at himself. Because, really, despite the uptight attitude, she was *everyone's* type.

Especially with those big blue eyes and soft mouth that made him think of deep, wet kisses in the dark. Maybe with a big fat harvest moon hanging in a midnight sky and bathing the street in a romantic glow. He could easily picture her beautiful features bathed in moonlight as she turned up her face for a kiss. His kiss.

Snorting softly at his uncharacteristically fertile imagination, Gabe decided he'd been in California too long if he was creating romantic movie scenes in his head.

She looked annoyed and maybe a little insulted, which dispelled his imaginary romantic scene. "What is your type?" she asked curiously, then, as though realizing what she'd said, grimaced. "No, don't tell me." She stomped up the stairs to her front door. "Blonde, stacked and vapid, right? And most likely a surgically enhanced beach bunny. *Yeesh.* Big surprise." She turned and glared at him. "Did you know that in ancient Greece, blonde hair was associated with prostitution?"

"Is that a fact?" Gabe grinned and realized with a jolt of surprise that he kind of liked the way she scowled at him—like a ruffled kitten ready to spit and scratch at the slightest move from the neighborhood mongrel. It made him want to reach out and stroke her until she arched into his caress and purred.

And as he'd never had any similar urges before, he decided that he'd slipped over the edge for real and should probably have himself committed.

"I thought the saying was blondes have more fun," he taunted, and chuckled when she snorted her opinion of his questionable taste in women…and in hair color.

"You're such a…a man," she growled in that oddly husky voice that did strange things to his gut. Shoving the key into the lock, she pushed open the door before throwing "Incapable of looking past bleached hair, a pair of large breasts and long tanned legs" over her shoulder. Then, without another glance in his direction, she disappeared into the building and slammed the door behind her.

For a long moment Gabe stared at the empty spot, gradually becoming aware of the growing lightness that had replaced his previous black mood. And when he realized he was grinning like a loon, he shoved a hand through his rumpled hair. He was vaguely surprised by his new neighbor's ability to make him smile when he hadn't felt like smiling in what seemed like forever.

Yet despite her prickly, less-than-friendly attitude, he kind of couldn't wait to see her again so he could tease an irritated scowl—or an adorable blush—to her face. Or maybe he just wanted to find out what other weird and wonderful facts she had tucked away inside that dark head.

He had a feeling she had one for every occasion.

With a cheerful whistle, Gabe turned and shoved his key in the lock and pushed open the door. "G'night, blue eyes," he murmured, before slipping inside. "Sweet dreams."

His day—and maybe the future—had just got a whole lot more interesting.

Holly's breath whooshed out noisily as she sagged back against the door. *Oh, boy,* she thought, feeling strangely buzzed and exhausted. And then, because she didn't know what else to think, she rolled her eyes, and said it out loud. "Oh, boy."

The sound of someone clearing their throat made her jump and squeak for the second time in as many minutes. Her gaze flew to where her friend and sometime housemate Tessa stood in the open doorway to the sitting room, watching her curiously. "You're late," Tessa accused lightly. "And you didn't answer your cell."

Dr. Enzo DellaToro, fiancé to a new housemate, Kimberlyn Davis, popped his handsome Italian head round the door. "She was getting ready to call the police."

"The police?" Holly squeaked, still feeling a little tongue-tied in his presence. "What for?"

He shrugged. "Maybe it's hormones."

Tessa waved that aside and folded her arms beneath her breasts. "Who were you talking to? I know for a fact that it's too early for Mr. Steiner to walk his dog."

Holly ducked her head. There was no way she could tell them about…well, him. Tessa would ask a million questions and try to set her up again and Holly was honest enough with herself to know that Gabriel Alexander was *way* out of her league. She'd learned a long time ago that guys who wore that casual confidence like a pair of soft well-fitting jeans mostly didn't even notice she existed. She was too serious, too quiet, too nerdy and…and boring.

Not to mention scarred.

"I'm sorry," she said with an apologetic grimace, "but did you know that the actual statistics for people going missing is lower than the reports?"

Enzo and Tessa exchanged silent looks and Holly hid a wince because she knew what they were thinking. Hoping she could head them off before succumbing to the guilty need to explain herself, she pushed away from the door and walked toward them, avoiding their searching gazes by focusing on the three large buttons on her jacket.

Ignoring the questions she could see Tessa was dying to ask, Holly led the way into the living room, where dinner was clearly under way.

"What happened?" Kimberlyn asked in her sexy Southern drawl before Holly could apologize for being late.

She felt her cheeks go hot and bit back a curse. Damn it. What was this, focus-on-Holly night? She tried for a casual "I don't know what you mean" only it emerged sounding defensive instead.

"You're flustered," Tessa, who'd known her the longest, said. "And you always come up with random facts when you're nervous."

"Nothing happened," Holly hastened to reassure them. "Not really. I…er…I just got home and there was a guy on the street."

"Is he still there?" Sam asked, wandering into the sitting room from the kitchen.

"Why didn't you use your mace?" Tessa demanded, and Holly laughed.

"Relax," she said, feeling her cheeks heat. "I, um…I didn't need to. It was the new neighbor."

"Ooh," Tessa said, eyes alight with curiosity. "Is he hot?"

Sam tapped the neck of the beer bottle thoughtfully against his lip. "Next door, huh?" he drawled, distracting Holly from asking Tessa what an almost married pregnant woman was doing checking out hot guys. "Isn't he the new cosmetic surgeon? The Hollywood guy?"

Holly blushed and gaped at him a little because it was the most she'd ever heard him say. She turned to throw her shoulder bag onto the nearest surface and shrug out of her jacket, hoping they hadn't seen that annoying tell-tale re-action that had haunted her adolescence.

"Yes…and it's, um…he's from…um, Beverly Hills." She rolled her eyes at herself. She'd gone for casual and ended up sounding like she had something to hide.

"Ooh." Tessa grinned, her eyes alight with glee. "She thinks he's hot."

She totally did.

"I do not!" Holly said defensively as she kicked her sandals off a little viciously. Her mother would have a fit to see the elegantly appointed sitting room littered with apparel. "Besides, sixty-five percent of men prefer surgically enhanced blondes with fake…tans, not pale brunettes who um…never…get…any…sun."

"Hey," Enzo and Sam objected simultaneously, both looking a little affronted by the "surgically enhanced blondes" quip. Holly rolled her eyes and huffed out a breath. Damn it, she was embarrassed enough, without getting into a discussion about blondes being more fun. Especially with Tessa—who knew a little about Holly's family—looking empathetic.

Better just to pretend it was no big deal. Because it hadn't been. *Really.* No big deal at all.

"Sorry, Enzo." She shrugged and sent Sam a look beneath her lashes because she'd seen a surgically enhanced blonde chatting him up at the hospital festival a few months earlier. She blinked innocently and added, "I was going to say he's okay if you like the tanned beach type. Which I don't."

"Oh, honey," Kimberlyn snorted. "Everyone does."

"Let's invite him to dinner," Tessa teased.

"No!" she practically squeaked, and Tessa laughed and threw herself into the nearest chair. She picked up a glass filled with what looked like mojitos from the sweating jug on the coffee table. "So-o-o," she said, sucking down a mouthful and licking her lips. "What's he like?"

Holly shrugged. "Okay, I guess," she lied blithely, and dropped onto the sofa, quickly releasing her hair from its high ponytail so it fell around her shoulders in a dark silky mass…hopefully hiding her expression. "And why are you drinking?"

"Oh, I'm not. Sam made me a virgin." There was a short pause as everyone absorbed that statement before Holly snorted.

"Won't Clay have something to say about that?"

Tessa's mouth curled and her eyes got that dreamy look Holly associated with people in love. The sappy one that made other women sigh with envy. "Of course he would." She waved aside Holly's attempts to change the subject. "Don't change the subject, Dr. Buchanan. Is he the tall, dark and handsome guy with blue eyes and a wicked smile?"

"That's your fiancé, Tessa," Kimberlyn pointed out, and Tessa blinked in surprise. Surprise that slid into a secret little smile, making her resemble a sleek cat that had recently swallowed a fat, juicy pigeon. "Oh, yeah, so it is. Lucky me."

Enzo snorted but Holly just felt relieved that their attention had finally shifted away from her. She exhaled with a soundless whoosh and reached for what was obviously the non-virgin jug of mojitos. She was in the process of pouring herself a hefty drink when she realized everyone had gone silent and was staring at her like she'd announced she was an alien from a distant galaxy who liked to suck guys' hearts out with a kiss.

"What?" She carefully replaced the jug, her gaze warily bouncing from one face to the other. "What's wrong?"

Behind Tessa's curiosity was concern. "Are you sure you're okay?"

Holly's brows wrinkled and she looked down at herself, half expecting to see her buttons open, that she was wearing a black bra under a white shirt or that she'd spilled something unmentionable on her blouse. Seeing nothing unusual, she looked up in confusion. "What?"

They all looked pointedly at the glass in her hand. "You're drinking cocktails now?" Tessa demanded, and Holly flushed, cursing Tessa's eagle eye and the realization that the encounter with their new neighbor had rattled her.

It had been bad enough that she had to see him at work, now she was probably going to fall over him every time she left her house too.

Instead of admitting that she was rattled, she shrugged casually, like she drank cocktails all the time, and sank back against the cushions with a sigh of relief.

Look at her, all sophisticated and casual.

"Well, since I'm not pregnant, I thought I'd stop being so predictable. Maybe I need to loosen up a little. Or…something. Anyway," she added quickly, as heat rose in her face, "it's been an exhausting day."

"You're acting weird," Tessa said, with a little frown. "What aren't you telling us?"

"Nothing. Really." Holly shrugged casually then exhaled a little shakily when she realized she hadn't sounded convincing even to her own ears. Maybe if she stuck with a half-truth they'd be satisfied and drop the subject. "Okay, it wasn't nothing," she confessed a little guiltily, and took a sip of mojito, grimacing at the strong taste of alcohol. *Yeesh, someone here had a heavy hand.* "I heard the code blue and full house call for OR three and went in to watch for a while."

A "full house" was the med students' term for a full trauma team consisting of all the main disciplines. It only rarely happened that a case needed so many specialists on urgent standby.

Suddenly ravenous, Holly snagged a large slice of pizza and between mouthfuls of crispy base, gooey cheese and spicy pepperoni she told them about the guy who'd fallen from construction scaffolding, thinking how amazingly clever she'd been to distract them.

Besides, she thought with a quiet huff of relief, they'd knocked back a couple of mojitos before she'd arrived and were already buzzing along quite nicely. Even Tessa, despite drinking the non-alcoholic version.

Although Holly rarely drank anything more lethal than white wine, she slugged down her first drink like it was medicine and found she kind of liked the tangy minty lime flavor and the way it made her lips tingle.

By the time her lips turned numb, so had her brain—which was great because it meant she could stop obsessing about her humiliating behavior and forget about the new neighbor.

So-o-o-o forgetting about the hot new neighbor.

Especially, she mused, surreptitiously fanning her hot cheeks, those embarrassing facts about blondes. Besides, if she wasn't his type, *he* most definitely wasn't *hers*.

Not by a long shot.

She tended to go for the serious business type. *He* was

too...um...the word *laid-back* came to mind and...and carelessly put together with an indolent, unconscious grace that made her feel like that clumsy awkward kid again.

Another thing that really annoyed her was his natural self-assurance. She would like to call it arrogance but it wasn't...not really. It was like he'd popped out of his mother's womb knowing his place in the world and didn't care if anyone disagreed. She had a feeling that air of casual affability hid a razor-sharp intellect. She'd seen ample evidence of a wicked sense of humor too and, *jeez*, she wished she didn't find that so attractive. Especially as it had being aimed at her most of the time.

Her cheeks grew hot when she recalled falling into his lap, only to find him huge and hard beneath her bottom.

She wasn't interested in him, she assured herself. He wasn't part of her plan—especially someone used to physical perfection. She was just annoyed to discover that after all the hard work she still hadn't outgrown the nerdy, clumsy adolescent that blushed and stuttered in the presence of a hot guy.

But later, when she slid between crisp, clean sheets and snuggled down into her pillow, along with a gently spinning room, Holly had a sudden and vivid image of a naked surf god sprawled across a sea of white on the other side of her bedroom wall. For the first time in her life she experienced a full-body flush that she promptly blamed on all those darn mojitos!

CHAPTER FIVE

WHEN SHE WAS stressed Holly sometimes had nightmares about the accident that had changed her life. She didn't often think about it but the following week she assisted a senior surgeon in repairing the face and torso of a maintenance worker who'd been caught in a gas explosion.

It had brought back memories of waking to a world of eerie silence filled with dust; the realization that she'd been unable to move and blinding pain when she'd tried.

She'd later learned that her face and right arm had been lacerated by flying glass as she'd been flung twenty feet from the exploding elevator car. The worst had been when she'd turned her head and seen the lifeless stare of a kid about her own age lying nearby. The sight of that empty eye socket where his merry brown eye had once been still haunted her dreams. One minute he'd been laughing and chatting with his friends, the next he'd been an unrecognizable bloodied mess.

Other than laceration injuries, she'd broken both arms and a collar bone and the ragged edges of her tibia had torn through the flesh of her right leg.

What she remembered most about the incident was the moaning and screaming.

Spooked by memories she hadn't thought of in years, Holly left the hospital and headed for the gym not far from West Manhattan.

Where other people enjoyed sweating and grunting through their workouts, Holly preferred the cool solitude of the pool. Besides, there was plenty of scientific evidence proving that submersion in water lowered blood pressure as well as stress levels. Besides relaxation, Holly liked the full-body workout swimming gave her. After the accident, it had been one of the physical therapy sessions she'd looked forward to and she'd eventually become a good swimmer.

And, boy, after the day she'd just had, she needed relaxation as much as she needed some alone time. Although she wouldn't have minded a little screaming to go with it, that wasn't on the cards. And until she landed the fellowship, the plan took precedence. Over everything.

She needed to do research for a paper she was writing on micro-surgical techniques but she was too wired to concentrate on anything and knew sleep would remain elusive if she went home. And recalling that what little sleep she'd managed lately had been filled with dreams of sun-warmed beaches, cool seas and…and hot surfers, Holly rolled her eyes because she was thinking of a certain hot celebrity surgeon. Again.

She dodged a couple necking on the stairs and entered the gym. Smiling a greeting at the girl manning Reception, she headed for the women's change room.

Within minutes she'd changed out of her street clothes and into her swimsuit. Scooping up her towel, she headed for the pool, hoping she would be alone. Alone meant she could get into her zone faster without having to dodge other swimmers. Alone meant she could get her workout done in record time and head home to food and her bed.

Okay, so she was also a little self-conscious about her scars, which were a lot more noticeable when she wore a swimsuit. Granted, they'd mostly faded but *she* knew they were there and in her mind's eye they were still livid and ugly.

Her heart sank a little when she saw the pool was already

occupied but after a few indecisive moments the need for the soothing feel of water closing over her head drove her onto the pool deck.

After a quick glance around, she realized that since the lone occupant appeared oblivious that he was about to have company, she could slip unnoticed into the water and pretend she was alone.

Dropping her towel over a nearby rail, she turned to face the clear blue water and wrestle with her hair. She twisted the heavy mass into a tight bun at the top of her head and secured it with a couple of holders as she approached the edge of the pool, taking a moment to admire the man's efficient, deceptively lazy style. He moved with the kind of fluid effortless grace only found in professional swimmers.

Pausing to stretch her tight muscles, she watched his long, tanned body power easily through the water toward her. Nearing the wall, he executed a languid racing turn as though it was as natural to him as walking. Fascinated, Holly followed the path his body made underwater until he surfaced some ten meters away, turning his head just enough to take advantage of his body's streamlining to breathe.

Darn, she thought with admiration as water glistened off his wide tanned shoulders and long powerful arms, she wished she could look half as good breathing, let alone swimming laps.

She spent another minute practically hypnotized by the dip and rise of wide shoulders and the shifting of muscles in a long tanned back until he abruptly disappeared in yet another turn at the opposite wall. Realizing she was standing transfixed by the sight of some guy doing nothing more interesting than swim up and down, Holly blinked as heat rose into her face.

What the heck are you doing, Holly? You came here to de-stress and get some exercise, not get all hot and bothered by some hunk out for his evening swim.

Feeling guilty for her somewhat racy thoughts, Holly took a deep breath and dived. Her foot slipped at the exact instant she realized she'd forgotten her goggles and instead of her usual graceful dive, she belly-flopped with a strangled shriek and sank like a stone.

The water was colder than she'd expected, closing over her head and rushing in on the heels of her startled gasp. For a few ragged heartbeats she panicked and flailed around like she'd forgotten how to swim, confused about which way was up. Just when she thought she'd run out of air, large hands clamped around her arms and hauled her upward.

Instinctively fighting the firm grip, Holly nearly lost what was left of the breath in her lungs when she was yanked roughly against a big hard body. They broke the surface in a tangle of limbs, gasping breath and gushing water.

"Jeez, lady," a deep familiar voice growled near her ear, and Holly's belly clenched before sinking as gracelessly as she had. "Are you trying to drown yourself?"

Gabe held the woman and waited while she spluttered and coughed, wondering if she'd pretended to drown, hoping to attract his attention. He'd had women do that and more, trying to get him to notice them.

It was only when she lifted her head and blinked huge dark blue eyes that he realized he was holding Holly Buchanan and she was staring at him like she'd suddenly found herself in the jaws of…well, Jaws.

"You?" she gasped.

He felt his mouth curl up at one corner and made no effort to release her. In fact, he drew her closer. "Well, well," he drawled softly, enjoying the feel of her body, still warm and incredibly smooth and soft, against his. The skin across his belly tightened in reaction. "What a…surprise. Are you by any chance stalking me?"

"Me?" she squeaked, her mouth round with outrage. "I was about to ask you the same thing."

"I was here first. Unless…" His eyes narrowed on her in mock suspicion. "Unless that was you hiding behind the pillar when I arrived earlier," he drawled, referring to the way he'd caught her ducking around corners or through the closest doorway when she'd seen him coming at the hospital.

Heat rushed into her face but she ignored his comment, her lips parting on a stuttered "I—I… Th-that was you? In the water, I mean?"

A frown tugged at Gabe's mouth at her incredulous tone. He wasn't sure she'd meant it as a compliment, which also meant she hadn't followed hoping to run into him. He ignored the odd feeling in his gut that couldn't possibly be disappointment.

"You sound surprised."

For a couple of beats she blinked myopically at him. It was fascinating to watch the conflicting expressions race over her features as if she couldn't decide if she was annoyed, impressed or embarrassed. It made him wonder what the heck was going through her mind to make her frown and blush.

"Not at all. It's just…" She suddenly blew out a breath and rolled her eyes. The idea that she'd been watching him was oddly satisfying, considering how much time he'd spent either thinking about her lately or watching her run for cover every time she saw him coming. Especially today, when evaluating her technique hadn't been the sole purpose of his presence in observation room six.

She licked her lips and he instantly forgot what he was thinking. "I…um…I didn't know you swam… At this gym, I mean."

His gaze dropped to her mouth and his skin tightened as heat gathered low in his gut. "And a good thing too or you might have drowned yourself."

"Don't be silly," she wheezed, lifting a hand to wipe moisture off her face. "I slipped, that's all. I'm an excellent swimmer."

He felt a chuckle rise in his throat. "Yeah? Then what was that incredibly graceful dive called? Because I can tell you I've seen preschoolers with more style than that."

She rolled her eyes. "The tiles are slippery," she muttered, dropping her gaze to his mouth. She sucked in a shuddery breath that pressed her breasts against his chest and made his eyes cross. It also made her realize she was plastered up against him like wet silk—okay, and maybe she'd discovered what the feel of her smooth warm skin was doing to him. She squeaked and tried to shove away but they were both slick and her hands kept slipping until she finally growled something that sounded like "Damn it, this is a nightmare" and managed to knee him in the thigh. He wasn't so sure that was an accident.

He muttered, "Wet dream is more like it."

She gasped and gaped at him. Her furious "*Ohmigod,* I can't believe you just said that" ended on a hacking cough, and Gabe shook his head as he slid his hands from her waist to lift her arms above her head even as she tried to take a swing at him.

"Come on, who didn't see that one coming?"

She choked and spluttered a bit more and he got kicked in the shin this time. He chuckled. "Breathe, Doc, before you hack up another lung or maybe knee me in the nuts."

"You…you deserve it," she croaked, when she could talk without spluttering.

He pulled back and dipped his head to peer into her face. "Is that any way to talk to the guy who just saved your life? For the fourth time, I might add."

"What are you doing here, *Dr.* Alexander?" she demanded in a husky voice that heated him up on the inside and gave him a few indecent thoughts. Thoughts he shouldn't be having about someone he was going to be working with. Thoughts about pushing her up against the side of the pool and practicing mouth-to-mouth.

"You mean, other than saving your sexy ass?"

Wild color rose beneath her creamy skin and Gabe was
seriously tempted to lean forward and lick her pink mouth—
see if she tasted as delicious as she looked.

"I'm perfectly capable of saving myself," she snapped,
and shoved at hands that had ended up very close to her
breasts—which were full and firm and incredibly entic-
ing in that skin-tight black sheath. Did she know their hard
points were practically begging for attention that he was all
too willing to give? "And let me go, damn it."

His blood heated in his veins at the thought of getting his
hands on her bounty and his grin turned mocking, as much
at himself than anything. He was mostly a leg and butt man,
probably because of all the boob jobs he'd performed. But
despite the number of breasts he had his hands on, none of
them had made a fraction of an impact on him compared
to Holly Buchanan's shrink-wrapped curves.

And he'd just this instant become a breast man too.

"Aww," he drawled, his voice a rough rasp filling the
inch separating them. "Do I have to?"

"No… Yes…I mean… *Damn it.*" Confusion chased annoyance and desire across her face as Holly put a couple
of inches between them. Despite the move making him
chuckle, the distance gave him an even better view. She
saw the direction of his gaze, looked down and with an out-
raged squeak slapped her arms across her chest, glaring at
him like he was a pervert for enjoying the view. "They're…
they're all me," she snapped. "In case you were wondering."

He chuckled. "Yeah, I can tell."

His gaze drifted up her throat, past her stubborn little
chin to her mouth, where he got stuck for a few heart-stop-
ping beats. He finally locked eyes with her…and got caught
up in the incredible dark blue depths surrounded by a heavy
fringe of dark spiky lashes. For an instant his world tilted
and then his heart rate spiked like he'd been zapped with
a cattle prod.

The hair on the back of his neck prickled and a shudder of pure panic stomped up his spine with size thirteen army boots. Blinking, he shoved shaking fingers through his hair. *What the hell?* Next thing he'd be spouting poetry or something equally cheesy—not to mention freaking embarrassing.

When just the thought of it made his nuts shrink, Gabe didn't know whether to be relieved or freaked out. *Jeez.* This was exactly what happened when a guy went without for more than six months, he told himself. He got caught up in sexy blue bedroom eyes and starved his brain of oxygen when his blood drained south of the border.

"Stop…stop looking at me," she rasped, turning away from his gaze. He blinked her face into focus, finally realizing his scrutiny was upsetting her and that she was a little hunched over as though to protect herself. From him? What the hell?

"What are you talking about?"

"I feel like a…a bug under a microscope."

"A very attractive *wet* bug," he interjected, and dropped his gaze in time to see her bite her lip. And because he hadn't eaten since noon, he was tempted to take a nibble too but she turned wounded eyes up to his and he froze. "What? What's wrong?"

"I'm d-damaged."

He laughed but when her expression turned fierce, like she wanted to slug him, he frowned, confused as hell because the woman was damn beautiful. The last thing he'd call her was damaged.

Stunning, sexy and hot? Yes. Snotty as hell? Definitely. Damaged? No way. Scars and all. There was too much elegant bone structure, stubborn chin and lush mouth for that.

Frustrated, he shoved a hand through his hair. "What the hell are you talking about?" He felt like one wrong move from him and she'd… Hell, he didn't know, just that he'd go crashing through the ice any second and be plunged into deep frigid waters. She glared at him and he felt like an insensitive jerk. He didn't have a clue why.

"I'm damaged, flawed, broken," she muttered fiercely. "Take your pick. I've heard it all before, and more. Including ugly."

"Ugly?" He made a sound of irritation. "Did someone tell you that?" he rapped out.

She lifted a hand to cover the pale thin scars and blinked at him warily. "I've got eyes. I know what I look like."

He reached out and wrapped his fingers around her wrist, gently pulling her hand away so he could study the thin silvery scars marring her creamy skin with professional interest and clinical detachment. He had a feeling anything else would offend her.

Through the delicate skin on the inside of her wrist her pulse beat a rapid tattoo. Even if he hadn't felt the racing heartbeat, he couldn't ignore the anxiety leaking from every pore.

She made a sound of distress in the back of her throat and tried to tug free but he held her easily, lifting his free hand to gently turn the scarred side toward him.

He wanted to lean forward and kiss each imperfection, run his tongue along the pale lines. "I don't think you do," he said mildly. "Have you heard of body dysmorphic disorder?"

She jerked her chin away and flashed him a scowl of outrage. "Of course I have. Are you suggesting I have BDD or that I'm vain?"

Gabe shook his head and sent her a faint smile. "Neither. I merely wondered if you knew about it. I'm not going to lie and say your scars are invisible, Holly, but I think they're more noticeable to you because you know they're there."

She rolled her eyes and tried to twist free but he ignored her, his large, warm hand holding her captive. "I know they're there," she said in a low, fierce voice, "because I had to live through the stares as well as the endless procedures to get rid of them."

"And…" he guessed, lightly tracing one thin line across the top of her cheekbone to where it disappeared into her hairline. She sucked in a breath and after a moment a tiny shudder went through her. Gabe had to steel himself against the urge to wrap his arms around her, offer his strength. "You remember what they were like when they were new," he pointed out gently. "But unless you deliberately did this to yourself, it's not your fault."

"Of course I didn't do it to myself,' she snapped, then sucked in a huge breath that was probably an attempt to calm her but which nearly gave Gabe a heart attack when the round globes of her breasts swelled above the neckline of her swimsuit. "It was…an accident."

He had to clear his throat twice and fight the overwhelming urge to drop his gaze to her plump curves and drool like a guy. "Well, from a cosmetic point of view, even *I* couldn't have done better."

She snorted. "Modest much, Dr. Alexander?"

He chuckled. "No. In Beverly Hills you have to be good or word gets around and the next thing you know you're in Tijuana, doing budget nip-and-tuck tourist deals. Switzerland or Germany?"

She tugged again on her wrist and because he was somewhat distracted he let her go. She immediately wrapped her arms around herself. He could have told her it was too late. *Waa-aay* too late. Now that he'd seen—and felt them pressed against his chest—he was sure the image was burned into his brain for all time. And why he found that sexier than if she'd been naked, he didn't know. Clearly he'd lost brain cells along with his testosterone leakage.

"Switzerland. How did you know?"

At the question his gaze rose from watching her mouth form words. He blinked in confusion and got lost in the smoky blue depths surrounding enlarged pupils.

"I, uh…" What the hell were they discussing? Oh, yeah,

he thought with a rush of relief—her scars. "I recognized the technique from a study I did in med school."

She looked back at him and her expression was as dazed as his had been a few seconds ago. Clearly she was also having difficulty keeping up with their verbal exchange when their bodies insisted on conversing on a whole different level. A level that left his skin tight, his blood pounding through his veins and his body in pleasurable pain like he was an addict suffering withdrawal.

Holly licked her lips and Gabe's blood went instantly hot. She must have recognized the look in his eyes because hers widened and she edged away, watching him warily.

"Stop that!"

"Huh? Stop what?"

"Stop looking and…and talking about my flaws."

"Everyone has flaws," he murmured distractedly, his body following hers like he was a divining rod and she was a hidden source of water. He caged her against the wall with his arms, his voice a rough, low sound between them that heightened the feeling of isolation and intimacy.

Slick, naked skin brushed, sending goose-bumps marching across his skin like an invading army, and the water separating them heated until he thought he saw steam but maybe that was just his brain smoking. "My one ear is higher than the other and I have big feet."

She gaped at him like he was a lunatic for equating big feet with trauma scars. "You're kidding, right?"

"No, I'm serious. I bet if you looked you'd probably find a lot more. Like I broke my nose when my surfboard smacked me in the face."

She grimaced sympathetically. "What happened?"

"I was sixteen and showing off," he sighed. "Instead of being impressed, the girl fainted when she saw blood and the rest of my summer was ruined."

Her eyes lightened, as Gabe had intended, and he wanted to close the distance between them and kiss her, tease a

smile to her lush mouth. He wanted to make her laugh—
really laugh. Not the polite little smile he'd seen her aim
at people she wanted to keep at a distance. Hell. He'd like
any kind of smile, considering all she ever did with him
was scowl.

"That's really tragic."

Yeah, about as tragic as a grown man behaving like a
sixteen-year-old.

He gave a wounded look. "It was a traumatic adolescent
experience that scarred me for life," he accused, when she
smothered a snicker. "Anyway, in addition to a broken nose,
my one eyebrow arches more than the other and an old girl-
friend told me I look permanently mocking."

"The one who fainted?"

"No." *Smartass.* "That one was history before I could
impress her with my manliness. It was another…girl."

"Well, you are mocking," she pointed out, and when his
lips curved up at one corner, her eyes dropped to stare at his
mouth and he knew she was as affected by their proximity
as he was. After a moment her gaze slid away a little guiltily
and when her tongue emerged to flick over her lips he felt
it all the way to his big feet—and every inch along the way.

"Maybe a little," he rasped, struggling to follow the conversation. "What I'm trying to say is that people are not
perfect."

"You haven't met my family."

"Why?"

The movement of the water bobbed them together and
their bodies bumped, skin brushing skin, soft curves against
hard. Her breasts brushed his chest, sending sensation zing-
ing through him until his back teeth ached with the effort
not to yank her against him and taste her soft mouth.

"My mother was a beauty queen," she was saying in a
husky tone, as though the accidental touch had affected her
too. *Damn.* Maybe he should move away. Maybe he should
get out of the pool and take a really cold shower until he

could breathe without inhaling the scent of her, move without the memory of her soft skin brushing against his.

But instead of getting the hell out of Dodge, he pressed a thigh between hers and shifted closer, until the plump curves of her breasts were pillowed against his chest and her thighs quivered and clenched around his. She made a little sound in the back of her throat that emerged as a gasping squeak and he nearly came out of his skin. It was so hot he was surprised the water didn't evaporate. It was so hot he felt the back of his skull tighten and his skin buzz.

She gulped and pressed herself against the wall before continuing. "She was…um…runner-up for Miss America and w-won Miss World that same year." She sucked in a breath. "She's beautiful and perfect. Like my sister Paige. Like my father and my brother Bryant."

Something tugged at his memory but when her tongue peeked out between her pink lips it vanished and all he could think about was tasting the moist pink pillows of flesh just beneath his mouth.

Maybe it was the hour or the fact that her eyes were heavy and smoky with the kind of need thundering through his own veins. But with her lips just below his and the smooth skin of her inner thighs making his gut clench with an almost violent need, he was powerless to do anything but slide his hand to the back of her neck and lower his head.

She gasped. "What are you…doing?"

Just before their lips touched, he murmured, "Proving how perfect you are."

Bare skin and thin elastane pressed into his belly and thighs. It flooded him with a need so powerful that he felt momentarily dizzy.

Oh, yeah, she was perfect all right. Perfect for him… perfect for his hands. Perfect for his mouth and he'd bet his grandfather's entire fortune she'd be perfect for his body too.

He reined himself in with difficulty but her breath hitched audibly in her throat and shot all his intentions—

to keep it light and teasing—straight to the bottomless pits of hell.

With a growl he covered her mouth with his in a kiss that instantly turned greedy and hot. He was thirty-five. A man who loved women; loved their bodies and the way their bodies felt against his. He loved the way they tasted and smelled and he loved the feel of their soft, firm flesh beneath his hands. He loved everything about them and he especially loved taking his time. But everything he'd ever learned about women went right out of his head the instant her mouth opened beneath his.

It was like he'd been sucked into a vortex created by her soft, wet mouth and soft, warm body and he couldn't think beyond getting more. More of her mouth, more of her silky curves pressed to the front of his jammer swimming trunks. More of her.

He pressed closer and when she uttered a breathy moan Gabe instantly took advantage and slid his tongue into her hot mouth. Without realizing he was doing it, he groaned low and deep in his throat and adjusted the fit of his mouth over hers, creating a light suction that made her whimper and arch into him, her hands clutching at his shoulders.

Blood roared through his head and he felt himself go under—submerged in liquid heat and drowning pleasure where his only lifeline was the feel of her soft mouth beneath his. And if he heard the alarm warning in the back of his mind, he ignored it in favor of murmured sighs that filled his ears and the slick, warm feel of her mouth beneath his.

Holly was aware of only two things. The big, hard body pressed to hers…the tangle of their limbs and the way his hand cradled her head as he devoured her resistance along with her breath. Okay, and she was also aware of the hard thigh between hers and the evidence of his arousal pressed almost painfully against her belly.

Her mind spun even as her eyes drifted shut and her

body softened, cradling that huge, hard shaft. He groaned. It came from so deep in his chest—like it'd been dragged up from the depths of his soul—that the responding vibrations swept through her like a subwoofer turned on high. And before she could remember her plan or think that maybe this was a very bad idea, she surrendered to the taste of him, greedily eating at his mouth and the hot, hungry kisses he fed her. Kisses that were deep and drugging and told her he was ravenous and that she was his next meal.

She'd never known kisses could be so hot or...hungry. Or that a man's mouth was capable of making her head spin, her belly dip and her body feel like one move and she'd go off like a bottle rocket.

And then there were no more thoughts as need and greed sucked her under, stole her breath along with any thoughts she might have to resist.

But there was no resisting the unstoppable force that was Gabriel Alexander and if she was honest with herself she didn't want to. Didn't want to push him away or stop the onslaught on her senses. Didn't want to resist his hot hardness sliding up to press against the apex of her thighs where she was hot and damp and aching with emptiness.

It was also wildly exciting to discover that someone like him could want her...with such rough urgency.

Then it didn't matter because all her thoughts drained away along with her breath, sucked out by his greedy mouth. But she found she didn't need breath as much as she needed this. This wild out-of-control feeling that sucked her under and sent her mind into a tailspin. And if she'd been in any condition to do anything but groan, slide her hands up the heavy muscles of his arms to his shoulders and press her body closer, she might have freaked at the ease with which he'd unraveled her defenses.

He fed her more deep, wet, hungry kisses that made her gasp and return them, just as hungrily, as if they were alone instead of in a public swimming pool where anyone might see them.

She didn't care. All she wanted was the hot, wet slide of his body filling the deep, empty ache within her. An ache she'd only discovered this very minute. An ache that she'd never thought existed, let alone experienced—especially in a brightly lit pool in central Manhattan.

He broke off the kiss to croak *"Damn,"* against her mouth and drag air into his heaving chest like he'd just sprinted three lengths of the pool without breathing. For several long beats they shared air until Holly lifted heavy lashes to see if he'd been as affected by the kiss as she had.

He looked a little shell-shocked. Kind of like she'd kneed him in the groin and he didn't know whether to throw up or pass out. Heck, she felt a little like passing out herself, and if she'd been in any state to do more than gulp air and cling to him, she might have panicked. Because...because, *damn*. Who'd have thought that Holly Buchanan would end up making out with Dr. Beverly Hills in a public swimming pool like a couple of randy teens? And want more? A whole lot more?

But her shock was about as little as the heavy evidence of his arousal, clearly outlined by his jammer suit practically shrink-wrapped to his lower body and visible beneath the water.

Okay, so she'd looked. It was better than seeing the hot blue-green eyes staring into hers until her thighs went up in flames. Her vision grayed at the edges and she thought she was having a panic attack until she realized she was holding her breath. She had to exhale or pass out.

And then he'd be forced to save her by performing mouth-to-mouth. *Oh, yes. Please.*

She must have swayed because his hands shot out to steady her. "You okay?" he rasped, and Holly stared up into his eyes and wondered why she'd never noticed how stormy they could get. Like the waters of the Caribbean stirred by hurricane winds.

"I…um…" And when nothing else emerged, he gave her a quick, hard shake to snap her out of her trance. But Holly was well and truly speechless. Who wouldn't be after that… that feeding frenzy?

"You going to pass out?" emerged rough and hoarse, as though he had as little control over his vocal cords as he had over his breathing. She inhaled and exhaled a couple more times until the urge to lose consciousness eased.

"Wh-a-at?"

A ragged chuckle scraped up from the depths of his chest and after a couple beats he shoved shaking fingers through his hair. "Damn it. I have to go." He sounded frustrated and a little like he was about to lose it. And, *oh, boy*, she could identify. "Are you going to be all right?"

"Oh…um…yes." She sucked in a couple more breaths and blinked up at him in confusion until she finally recognized the beeping noise she'd thought was the little warning sound in her head.

He was being paged and she hadn't even heard it over the pounding in her ears. Her head cleared a little more and she blew out a ragged "Go."

CHAPTER SIX

HOLLY WASN'T ABOUT to tell him that she felt like someone had smacked her against the head and left her ears ringing. She wasn't about to admit that every muscle in her body trembled—either with unfulfilled need or shock at her own behavior.

She white-knuckled the side of the pool with one hand and lifted unsteady fingers to her tingling lips, watching with dazed eyes as he hauled himself onto the pool deck. She felt shaken to her core. Kind of like finding out that aliens existed and that the government was helping them experiment on humans in return for their technology. Only… more.

Holy cow. Who knew anyone could kiss like that? Kiss *her* like that? As though he'd wanted to swallow her whole.

Water gushed down his body as he rose to his full height and she finally got a good look at what he'd been hiding beneath his jeans and sweatshirts—everything his jammer suit was supposed to cover, but didn't. *Gulp.*

She didn't realize her mouth had dropped open until he turned and caught her ogling his tight butt. His brow—the one that was usually arched in subtle mockery—rose up his forehead and a little lopsided grin sent that dimple creasing the lean planes of his cheek.

Oh, God. He'd caught her in the act of ogling him like he was a delicious pastry.

"Are you going to be okay? I hate leaving you alone when you're not such a great swimmer."

Holly's blush turned to a grimace at the reminder of her graceless dive. She didn't know what was worse—being caught leering at the goodies or...or having him witness her clumsiness. Again.

"I'm fine, Dr. Alexander. I...uh, slipped, that's all." She rolled her eyes as he wound a huge towel around his waist, his arched brow probably questioning her sudden attack of professionalism. But it was either that or drown herself at the memory of the way she'd whimpered and clutched at him like she'd been starving and he'd been a chocolate fudge sundae. "Maybe I'm not in your league, but I can hold my own."

"Uh-huh," he said, like he didn't believe her, and shoved fingers through his wet hair. Droplets showered around his head and shoulders and Holly felt equal amounts of glee and astonishment when she noticed his hands were shaking.

"I'm a great swimmer."

"If you say so." His phone started ringing and he grunted, looking for a moment like he'd love to toss the thing in the pool. But surgeons on call didn't have that luxury. "Look, I've gotta go. Promise me you'll be okay."

She rolled her eyes again, secretly pleased by his obvious reluctance to leave—although that might have something to do with his inability to walk in his...uh, condition. She bit her lip and watched his eyes go dark.

"I promise I'll be okay," she said hastily, and he finally sighed and gathered up his stuff.

He paused to send her one last look from beneath heavy, aroused lids. "A rain-check on the...other thing."

Holly shivered and dropped lower into the water to hide her body's reaction and stop her suit from melting beneath that laser-bright gaze. "The...thing?" One corner of his mouth curved and her breath caught in her chest. "Oh."

She swallowed hard and clenched her thighs together. "You mean…the, um…kiss?"

His grin turned wicked and his eyes burned a molten blue-green as they slid over her exposed skin, setting fire to her hair and her thighs. Jeez. It was a good thing she was submerged in water or her swimsuit—along with her thighs—would be history. "Oh, yeah," he rasped, his voice a dark slide of sin against her sensitized nerve endings as he turned and headed for the exit. "The kiss."

And just before he disappeared through the door she heard him say, "Definitely going to be another kiss."

And because he sounded so sure of himself—so arrogantly sure of *her*—she called out, "Don't hold your breath, Dr. Alexander. That was simply a thank-you for saving me." His response was deep laughter that floated across the pool and went straight to all her happy places that were feeling decidedly unhappy…and frustrated, *darn it*.

"Keep telling yourself that, Dr. Buchanan," rang in her ears, and Holly stared at the door for a few moments more before shaking her head as though to dispel the images lodged there. Sucking in a shuddery breath, she looked down to check that she was still clothed and wasn't sporting singe marks on her skin.

She was surprised to find that her suit hadn't vaporized and that the water hadn't boiled her like a lobster. Puffing out her cheeks, she blew out air in the hope that she could dispel the bubbles lodged in her brain. Because it was the only reason that would explain her wanton behavior. Especially with a man like Gabriel Alexander. A man who'd dedicated himself to the pursuit of perfection. A man who wasn't blind enough to ignore just how imperfect she was.

After a few moments getting her breathing under control, Holly squared her shoulders and sank beneath the water, ignoring the muscles trembling in her limbs like she'd just stepped off a carnival ride.

It was time to douse the fire and get into her zone, she

told herself firmly. A zone that didn't include sexy Hollywood surgeons with hot eyes, hard bodies and big warm… hands.

She had barely found her rhythm and was approaching the wall to turn when movement caught her attention. Stopping abruptly, she reared out of the water, her gaze automatically taking in a pair of battered sneakers at the edge of the pool.

She followed the long line of jeans-clad legs, over the bulge of a button fly and up a wide expanse of black T-shirt-covered chest to a tanned neck and square jaw gleaming with gold-tinted stubble. Stubble, she recalled with a shudder; that had scraped against her skin with rough eroticism.

She was surprised to see him. Dropping her head back, she quickly submerged then rose, lifting both hands to smooth her hair off her face. When she opened her eyes she found he'd dropped to his haunches and was looking hot and cool all at once. Their eyes met and a wild flush raced over her flesh at the memory of what he could do with his mouth.

"I thought you left?"

He shook his head. "I need you," he said, and the flush became a shudder, along with tightening breasts and clenching belly. Momentarily stunned, she gaped up at him as though he'd suggested something hot and forbidden…and incredibly tempting.

"I… You… What?"

He must have correctly interpreted her confusion because his mouth curved and that darned dimple made an appearance in his tanned cheek. "That'll have to wait for another time, Dr. Buchanan." He laughed and held out a hand as though he expected her to take it. Holly looked at his big brown hand and got a little dizzy just thinking about how it made her feel.

"Wha-at?"

He chuckled. "Pay attention, Doctor. I need you to get

out of the pool and get dressed. The hospital can't reach Dr. Frankel and we urgently need another surgeon. You're it."

"I'm not a maxillofacial surgeon."

"Close enough," he said a little impatiently, and waggled his fingers.

Without questioning him further, Holly took his hand and the next instant she was standing beside the pool, swaying a little on wobbly legs as water gushed down her body. He wrapped her towel around her shoulders and nudged her toward the exit.

"You have five minutes to change while I call a cab."

Holly walked into the gym lobby with a minute to spare to find Gabriel propped casually against the wall, laughing and chatting up a couple of women dressed in gym wear that looked three sizes too small. Both women looked taut and toned enough to bounce a coin on their tight butts and abs. And because she would never be able to do that, Holly was grateful her designer trousers and jacket covered her from the neck down.

The instant he saw her Gabe pushed away from the wall and wrapped his fingers around her elbow. The smile he aimed her way was warmly intimate as he called a quick "Night" over his shoulder. It also left her a little confused.

"Thank you," he murmured, steering her toward the automatic doors.

"For what?"

"For saving me from the barracudas." Oh, well, that certainly explained that, she decided with a pang that wasn't really disappointment. That smile hadn't been for her at all. Curious, she looked back over her shoulder and decided they did kind of resemble a couple of barracudas trawling the reef for a quick snack.

And to a woman who hadn't eaten all day, Gabriel Alexander was kind of snack-worthy.

"You looked like you were having a great time."

"Seriously?" He scowled at her as the doors swished

closed behind them. "Did you see how ripped they were? I was worried the blonde would wrestle me to the floor and put me in a headlock." *Or a something lock.* Holly hid a smirk. "It's humiliating," he muttered. "Besides, I don't like women who are so obsessed with the way they look they can't relax and have a good time."

The look he sent her made her hair smolder and her belly dip and quiver. "Women are supposed to be…soft," he murmured wickedly, his hot gaze dropping to her breasts. "Not have muscles in places they shouldn't. It makes a guy feel inferior."

He opened the cab door and stepped aside for Holly to get in. She couldn't see him feeling intimidated by anyone, let alone a couple of hot, sculpted gym bunnies. He'd have to care what people thought about him and he didn't strike her as a guy who worried overly much about that.

He got in behind her and she sneaked a peek out the corner of her eye when his thigh pressed against hers and their shoulders bumped. It sent warm little tingles of awareness pricking her skin.

She shifted over a little.

God, he was big, his wide shoulders taking up space she wasn't used to sharing with anyone and dominating it with a kind of smoldering masculine aggression that made her feel small and fragile when she looked most men in the eye.

By the time they arrived at the hospital Holly was wondering if she'd made a mistake by agreeing to accompany him after that kiss. She needed at least a week—okay, maybe a month…or three—to recover her equilibrium and stop wanting to either run for cover or…or jump his bones. Jumping his bones would be bad. Bad for the plan and bad for her heart.

"Get suited up and meet me in room two," he said briskly, with none of the misgivings or embarrassment she was experiencing. But, then, he was a guy. Kissing women and then going on to remodel a few breasts and thighs was all in a day's work. For her...? She sucked in air and let it out slowly. Well, not so much.

That kiss had been—

"You okay?"

Startled, she looked up into Gabriel's handsome face. "Of course." But instead of sounding coolly professional, she just sounded stunned and unsure. He must have thought so too because his eyebrow arched toward his hairline. "I'm fine, Dr. Alexander," she said, this time managing cool and confident, although it cost her. "But you might want to order me a glass of fresh orange juice. I can't remember the last time I ate."

One corner of his mouth curled. "I'll see what I can do. I'd hate for you to fall at my feet."

Holly rolled her eyes and hurried into the women's locker room. Falling at his feet was a habit she was determined to break.

She grabbed a pair of light blue scrubs, wondering how soon she would be permitted to wear the dark blue scrubs worn by all senior surgeons. It would be the final sign that she had reached the goal she'd work for years to achieve.

But there wasn't time to think about that now.

She quickly changed and headed for OR two, where the team would already be assembled. A ripple of anticipation tripped up her spine when she wondered what was waiting for her because she was fairly certain it would not be anything remotely cosmetic. Plastic surgeons didn't get called out for boob jobs or tummy tucks. Not at eight o'clock at night.

Maybe this would be her chance to show her real skills.

Already scrubbed, Gabe stood patiently while an OR nurse tugged the surgical gown over his shoulders and fastened the rear ties. Holly drank from the bottle of orange juice he'd ordered for her and waited for her turn to scrub up. When she'd finished she dropped the empty bottle into the trash and moved toward the basins.

He slid his gaze from the top of her dark head over the curvy body hidden beneath her scrubs, down her long legs to her surgical booties. Despite the outfit, she looked elegant and composed.

His gaze returned to her face and he frowned at the sight of her swollen lips. Lips he'd practically eaten off her face in his eagerness to taste that wide, lush mouth. Heat crawled up the back of his neck at the memory of the way he'd kissed her—like a green untried adolescent with his first crush. *Jeez.* It was no wonder she'd been stunned speechless. He'd been about as smooth as the Sawtooth Mountains.

"Is something wrong, Dr. Alexander?"

Realizing the nurse was addressing him, Gabe said, "Huh?" and tore his gaze from Holly. *Damn it.* He was standing here staring at her like a lovesick teen stunned stupid by big blue eyes and kiss-swollen lips.

"Is something wrong?" the nurse repeated, and Gabe dropped his gaze to her brown eyes for a moment before shaking off his odd mood. *Yep. Something* is *wrong. I'm wondering if I've lost my mind.*

"Just mentally preparing myself," he told her crisply, sliding one last hooded look at Holly and backing up to the swing doors. "Ready, Dr. Buchanan?"

Holly turned toward him, her face composed and serene as though that searing kiss hadn't happened. Then he caught a quick glimpse of her eyes before her lashes swept down and he realized she was fighting embarrassment and maybe apprehension. Whether for the upcoming procedure or the fact that he'd recently had his tongue in her mouth… he wasn't certain. Only that she avoided any eye contact as she brushed passed him and stepped into the sterile environment.

"Where do you want me?"

* * *

Three hours later Gabe lifted his eyes from where Holly's deft hands skillfully carried out his brisk instructions and recalled her last words.

Where do you want me? He could have told her that he'd have her anywhere he could get her but everyone was listening with big ears and he didn't want to provide fodder for gossip. He had a feeling Holly would do anything to avoid attention.

Over the last couple of hours he'd watched her carefully and couldn't suppress his admiration for her surgical skills. Watching from the observation room hadn't quite given him a sense of her abilities despite the video footage of other procedures he'd watched. He preferred the up-close-and-personal approach...of observation, he hastily amended. Working side by side with surgical residents gave him a better idea of their knowledge, skill and their surgical temperament. Despite what people thought, Gabe believed the difference between a good surgeon and an excellent one lay in their ability to stay calm and motivate people without resorting to temper tantrums or abuse. And he was pleased to discover that Holly's surgical temperament complemented his.

She was also a quick study. Calm and steady in a crisis, she didn't hesitate to follow his murmured instructions. In fact, she instinctively seemed to know what he would do next and was poised waiting for his cue or quickly moving in to assist when he'd appreciate another pair of hands attached to his brain.

The patient had been through massive facial trauma and ended up in reconstruction to stabilize his facial bones before something shifted and ended up in his brain.

Gabe had used a new technique he'd been developing to keep shattered bones stable while the swelling subsided enough for further reconstruction.

By inserting an ultra-thin malleable mesh beneath the

bones and over a specially made saline bag that would mold the cheekbone, he'd re-sculpted the facial bones to approximate the uninjured side. He'd explained that he was attempting to reduce the need for unnecessary additional re-construction, especially in heart patients. He'd only used the procedure once before, on a teenager who'd fallen off his snowboard and shattered his nose and both cheekbones. He'd had to resort to pins and wires to reconstruct the lower jaw, but the cheekbones had healed nicely with the new procedure, which included experimental bone-generating injections.

Once he was satisfied with the position and shape of the mesh-encased bone, he and Holly began the complex task of reattaching and re-forming the tendons in the jaw. It was tedious, painstaking work, requiring each connective bundle to be stretched and sewn onto its counterpart.

When he finally ordered the area closed with acelluar mesh, he could see Holly was exhausted but wildly buzzed. She'd just assisted in a ground-breaking procedure that was a first at WMS and had done remarkably well with the un-familiar procedure. The patient would still need ear, nose and lip reconstruction but that was for some time in the fu-ture when he'd healed from his other injuries and they could harvest skin and adipose cells.

They were finally wrapping up when Gabe noticed a tiny tremor move through her hands. She'd been on her feet since early morning and this had been her third lengthy proce-dure for the day. His gaze snagged hers, recalling how she'd gulped down the orange juice. But that had been hours ago and even he was ravenous.

"You okay there, Dr. Buchanan?"

Startled by the personal question after hours of imper-sonal orders and directions, she blinked a few times before nodding and dropping her gaze to where she was complet-ing the wound closure.

"Any special instructions?" Her voice was low and confident and Gabe relaxed, stepping back from the action. Rolling the two sets of latex gloves off his hands, he smiled behind his face mask.

"You're doing fine," he murmured, dropping the latex into the medical waste bin. "I'll leave you to finish things while I write up a report and send instructions to ICU." And with a quick word of thanks and congratulations to each member of the surgical team, he left the room, stripping off his gown, mask and bandana.

Leaving her to supervise the final stages was an unspoken vote of confidence that everyone in the room understood. It was well deserved. She might be an adorable klutz in her personal life but there was nothing clumsy about the way she handled herself in surgery. She just needed to believe in herself—go with her gut instinct. She knew what she was doing and she was good. He felt confident that with practice, expert guidance and encouragement she would become a highly skilled professional.

A half-hour later he spotted her heading across the hospital lobby toward the huge glass entrance. It was almost two in the morning and he was tired but knew from experience that he wouldn't sleep. He was still buzzing with adrenaline and though he usually preferred to be alone after a challenging procedure, he suddenly yearned for company.

Holly Buchanan's.

The realization that he was actively seeking out the company of a woman who usually went out of her way to avoid him was a little disturbing. He shook off the unwelcomed thoughts. This was just a post-operative conversation between colleagues.

That's all.

He quietly came up behind her, ignoring the fact that he didn't quite believe it himself. "Wanna share a cab?"

Startled, she jolted and flashed a look across her shoulder that could only be interpreted as guilty—especially when her gaze slid away from his and color seeped beneath her creamy skin.

Gabe wondered what she'd been thinking and if it had been about him. It wasn't ego that prompted the thought, he told himself, because he rarely obsessed about women or wondered if they obsessed about him. In Holly's case it was only fair considering the number of times he'd been distracted by the scent of her, teasing his senses over the antiseptic smells of the OR.

"I don't know. Are you going to leave me on the sidewalk if I say no?"

He chuckled and steered her through the automatic doors with a hand to the small of her back. "Not this time." Her sideways look was loaded with suspicion despite the shiver he felt go through her at his casual touch. "Promise. Scout's honor."

"I don't believe for a minute that you were a Scout."

"Hey, I'm a helpful kind of guy," he cut in, stepping off the curb and lifting his arm when he spotted a lighted cab half a block away. "Just ask my mom. And I'm always prepared."

"For what?" Holly asked beside him.

He shrugged. "For anything. Everything."

"Like what?"

He paused for a couple of beats like he was seriously considering her question then a wicked glance across his shoulder prompted a raised eyebrow. "Like paying close attention to expiration dates."

She huffed out a startled laugh as the cab pulled up, her look filled with censure for bringing up the condom incident. "With all your surgically enhanced beach bunnies, I would hope so," she said primly as he stepped forward to open the rear door. "They probably don't last long enough *to* expire."

"That's not entirely true," he drawled as she slid across the seat and gave the cabbie her address. He wondered what she would say to the news that his most recent stash had been dangerously close to expiration or that he hadn't thought about replacing them. Which was about as pathetic as his need for her company. Besides, he'd been in a relationship when his mother had been diagnosed. A relationship that had tanked faster than the *Titanic* the second the woman had found out he was thinking of giving up his lucrative practice to move east.

He'd been somewhat preoccupied and had completely missed the signs that she'd already transferred her affections to one of the other partners. When she'd thrown it in his face in a fit of pique, it had just reinforced the notion that he wasn't relationship material. And when all he'd felt had been relief, he'd known then it was time for him to move on. Besides, with his mother gone, there was nothing keeping him in California.

Holly's eyebrows rose up her smooth forehead. "Planning to live dangerously?"

Recalling that they were talking about his stash, Gabe chuckled and slid in behind her. "Hell, no. I have no intention of being caught in that particular web of lies and deceit."

Her eyebrows rose in surprise. "Lies and deceit?"

"Do you know the lengths some women are prepared to go to snag themselves a rich doctor husband?"

"As a matter of fact, I do. It's a common enough problem in med school, even though most med students have huge study loans to pay off and won't make any money for years."

"Yeah." He shuddered. "I had a brief moment of terror in my fourth year that turned out to be a false alarm but a couple of buddies weren't so lucky. One is already divorced and the other heading that way fast." He watched the purity of her profile in the lights off Broadway and wondered at her belief that she was imperfect. Everyone was imperfect. It was what made people interesting.

He recalled something she'd said about her family and

wondered if it had anything to do with her scars. But that was probably just speculation from his dysfunctional perspective.

"What about you?"

She turned toward him and his eyes slid over the elegant lines of her face gilded in warm gold from the streetlights. He'd like to say his examination was purely professional but he'd be lying.

"What about me?"

At this angle her scars were in shadow and he caught his breath at the stark beauty of her bone structure. He knew a lot of women who would kill to look like Holly Buchanan, scars or no scars. In fact, they just made her more interesting and...alluring, especially with emotion simmering in her eyes or when they darkened to a deep smoky blue when she was aroused.

He tried to stretch out his legs and ended up pressing his thigh firmly against hers. Heat gathered where they touched and the slight tremor he felt zip through her sent arrows of hunger and need into his belly until his jaw ached and his skin felt tight.

"Did you have to fight off party animals eager to marry a beautiful rich doctor and live a life of leisure?"

Her mouth dropped open and he could see he'd shocked her. Whether by the beautiful and rich statement or fighting off men, Gabe couldn't tell.

"You're kidding right?"

"Actually, no. I've lost count of the number of guys I've seen checking you out."

She laughed, her genuine amusement filling the interior with warmth.

The sound settled into his gut alongside the clawing lust and made him stare. *Damn.* She should laugh more. It transformed her from merely quietly beautiful to breathtaking, and filled her eyes with warmth and light. She seemed suddenly *alive*. As if she'd forgotten her plan, forgotten to be serious and was simply living in the moment.

He wondered if she'd always been so serious or if her "perfect" family had somehow squashed the life and joy out of her. And the sudden impulse to bring her joy made the hair rise on the back of his neck.

Whoa. A trickle of unease slid down his spine like a drop of icy water. Since when did he fall over himself to make women happy? Maybe he was just tired and hungry. Maybe he just needed a shower, food and about twelve hours of sleep.

She sent him a sideways look filled with mischief and he swallowed. Hard. *Holy crap.* The back of his neck tightened and his chest clenched. *This is bad. Very bad.*

"You're a funny man," she said, her eyes sparkling like deep sapphires.

His eyes dropped to her lips, curved in merriment, and he thought, *Oh, yeah. I'm hungry, all right.* But it wasn't for food. "Maybe you should do stand-up comedy." He opened his mouth, although he had no idea what he was going to say.

"Huh?" was about the sum total of his brainpower.

"People stare at scars, Dr. Alexander," she pointed out gently. "You, of all people, should know that. It's what keeps plastic surgeons in business."

What he did know was that when she spoke, all he could concentrate on was her mouth…and her eyes. The rest just faded away, retreated to the edges of his mind. Okay, maybe not faded because he was always aware of her soft, curvy body, but he didn't see scars. He was too busy fighting the urge to yank her into his lap and study the shape of her with his hands and mouth.

"And maybe you should be more observant."

"What's that supposed to mean? I'm very observant."

"Uh-huh." The cab turned and headed into Brooklyn. Gabe shifted in the seat to relieve the growing tightness behind his button fly but he knew he was fighting a losing battle. With every breath he took, her subtle feminine fragrance filled the cab and flooded his senses. It made him feel a little drunk.

Maybe it was just exhaustion.

He *hoped* it was just exhaustion.

The cab finally pulled up in front of her brownstone and he let out a relieved breath that he could escape before he did something he'd regret.

Like pull her into his lap and suck on that lip. Or run his hands under her snug little jacket to her soft, silky skin and lush curves.

"I'll get that," he said when Holly reached into her purse for the fare. He pushed open the door and slid from the cab. "Consider it payment for leaving you stranded the other night."

CHAPTER SEVEN

HOLLY SCRAMBLED FROM the cab, bumping the door closed with her hip. Gabriel straightened and stepped back from paying the cabbie and she had a flash of him as he'd looked earlier in Theatre. Tall, steady and *hot*—despite the laid-back charm he'd dispensed with equal measure to everyone on his team.

Although she'd deliberately avoided any opportunity to observe him in action, she could readily understand why the surgical nursing staff fought to be on his team. Other than the obvious hotness factor, he was patient and quick to break any tension with supportive praise or a few wise-cracks. He controlled the proceedings and the people around him with such skillful ease that everyone practically fell over themselves to please him.

Even her, she admitted with a frown. She could scarcely believe how they'd worked together—perfectly in sync—like they'd been doing it together for years instead of just a few hours.

It had been a little unnerving to discover that the man she'd been ready to dislike simply on principle wasn't the spoiled Hollywood celebrity she'd been expecting. And he was good, damn it. Good at kissing and making the breath catch in her throat. Good at making her forget the plan, and really good at saving a man's shattered face. So good that she couldn't help the little niggle of jealousy at the way he made things look so easy when she had to work so darned hard.

Sighing, she watched the cab disappear around the corner. A chilly wind had kicked up a few fall leaves and she shivered, hunching into her thin jacket as she looked up into a clear night sky. The moon was large and fat and seemed closer to the earth than usual and the halo around it promised a cold winter ahead.

She usually hated winter but for some reason it made her think of half-empty bottles of wine, a roaring fire and the flash of naked limbs and satisfied sighs. Her pulse leapt and heat rose from deep in her belly until it surrounded her in a shimmering glow—like a banked fire smoldering in her core, just waiting to burst into flame.

Puffing out her cheeks, she rolled her eyes because... because the tangle of limbs in her vision belonged to her and...and...

Another shiver moved through Holly.

She was in trouble.

Big trouble.

Spooked by her realization as much as the wildly erotic visions in her head, she turned and caught him watching silently from a few feet away. And in that instant her perception of him underwent yet another metamorphosis.

With only one side of his face starkly lit by moonlight and the rest in deep shadow, he looked big and bad and a little dangerous. Like a fierce golden angel banished from the heavens for inspiring illicit thoughts and needs in mortal women.

Gone was the laid-back flirt as well as the brilliant innovative surgeon with a knack for getting the best out of everyone. In his place was a man seemingly shrouded in mystery and...and aching loneliness.

The image made her heart squeeze in her chest and she had to resist the urge to go to him, press close to his big body and chase away the shadows she sometimes saw in his eyes.

But Gabriel Alexander was big and bad and beautiful and he certainly didn't need her. He didn't need anyone—especially someone scarred and focused on reaching her goals.

Shrugging off the uncomfortable realization that he was more than the hot, sexy Hollywood celebrity that made her tingle in hidden places, Holly became aware of the intensity of his gaze. His utter stillness unnerved her. She opened her mouth and said, "Did you know that Neil Armstrong was a Boy Scout?" before she could stop herself. "In fact, seventy one percent of astronauts," she continued determinedly, "are believed to have been Scouts."

His mouth curved, dispelling the image of a remote celestial being, and for once Holly didn't care if she sounded like a crazy person. She'd hated seeing that remoteness surrounding him like a thick, impenetrable cloud.

She bit her lip at the memory of the way his mouth had felt closing over hers. Of the way it had created a light suction that had made her breath hitch and her bones melt. She shivered again and this time it had nothing to do with the chill wind blowing from the north, announcing that winter was on its way.

Exactly what her shiver *was* announcing, Holly couldn't tell. Only that it made her heart pound, her skin tingle and her knees wobble like she'd tossed back one too many mojitos on an empty stomach.

"How did we get from being stranded in New York City to Neil Armstrong?"

"The moon, Boy Scouts…" she said a little breathlessly. "It seemed…I don't know…logical." She was helplessly caught in his eyes and the web of heat and tension that surrounded them. A tension that grew thicker by the minute, stealing her oxygen and her bones.

Her stomach chose that instant to growl loudly and she pressed a hand against the rumble, hoping he hadn't heard. But then it dawned on her that her weird dizziness—and possibly the hallucinations of lonely celestial beings—was simply a matter of low blood sugar. Her breath rushed out in a noisy whoosh of relief. *Oh, thank God,* she thought dizzily. All she needed was a quick meal, about ten hours of sleep and she'd be back to normal.

Whew. She gave a husky laugh that sounded a little too hysterical for comfort and headed for the steps leading to her house. *What a relief.*

She opened her mouth to call out goodnight and gave a surprised yelp when Gabriel took her elbow and steered her away from her brownstone.

Toward his.

"What…what are you doing?"

"Hmm?"

"That's your house, Dr. Alexander, not mine."

"I know, and don't you think we're past the stage of calling each other doctor?"

She wasn't going to talk about the kiss and calling him Dr. Alexander helped remind her that he was a colleague. She tugged on her elbow and growled when he ignored her attempts and continued to steer her calmly across the sidewalk, up the stairs past the late-blooming flowers in pots to the heavy wooden door. "Gabriel…why are you taking me to your house?"

The overhead light illuminated his features, revealing a wicked grin and gleaming eyes. She gave a mental eye roll. *Yeesh, so much for the lonely celestial being image.* He looked more like a fallen angel hell-bent on mischief and mayhem.

"Well," he said, fishing his keys from his pocket one-handed and jiggling them till he found the one he wanted. "I'm going to cook." He shoved the key in the lock.

She couldn't have been more surprised. "But…it's after one in the morning."

He arched that mocking brow at her and pushed open the door, drawing her closer despite her obvious reluctance. "You have a meal waiting for you?"

Hovering uncertainly on the threshold, she tugged on her arm and sent him a look filled with feminine exasperation when he tugged her closer instead. "Well, no, but…"

He drew her all the way in and shut the door, instantly surrounding them in deep silence that only emphasized her unsteady breathing and fraying nerves. "You haven't lived till you've sampled my…er…omelets." His grin flashed in response to her squeak as though he knew her mind had descended into the gutter. "Relax. I'll feed you and send you home. Scout's honor."

"I thought we'd established that you were never a Scout."

"No." He chuckled. "You established that."

Holly chewed nervously on her bottom lip as she looked around at the boxes still littering the floor. Not knowing what to do with her hands, she smoothed them over her thighs to disguise their trembling. "Maybe I should—"

He lifted a long tanned finger and placed it gently on her lips. "Food first." His touch made them tingle and she had to fight an overwhelming urge to open her mouth and lick him. Or maybe nibble on that long tanned digit.

She sucked in a sharp breath. *Holy cow.* She'd never had that kind of impulse before, which either meant low blood sugar was making her hallucinate or…or she was headed down a one-way street to disaster. She knew exactly which one *she'd* put her money on but hoped like hell she was just hallucinating.

His eyes gleamed as though he knew what he was doing to her, and in addition to her growing sense of looming disaster was an impulse to bite.

Huh.

Maybe she was just hungry after all.

"It's the least I can do after hijacking you at the gym."

At the mention of the gym, her face went hot and a little voice in the back of her head told her to run and keep running until the memory of those few minutes faded.

But he was taking her shoulder bag and briefcase hostage and to cover her tripping pulse she turned her attention to the furniture dotting the space not taken up by boxes.

It looked like one-tattoo-for-every-skirmish guy had simply dumped everything in Gabriel's sitting room and left.

"Interesting décor," she murmured, thinking there weren't even drapes at the windows and he'd been living here, what…three weeks already? But she'd seen his schedule and he'd probably only had time to come home, shower and sleep before returning to the hospital.

A glance over her shoulder caught Gabriel's grimace as he dropped her bags onto the nearest box. He pulled his black hoodie over his head, briefly exposing his flat, tanned belly before dropping the garment over her briefcase. The stark white T-shirt tested the seams of his shoulders and stretched across his chest, emphasizing the depth of his tan and the width of his biceps. She dropped her gaze to where she'd seen that flash of taut, tanned flesh and wondered why the brief sight of his belly button had seemed so…intimate. More intimate somehow than his earlier kiss. The one that had sucked the breath from her lungs along with her mind and any thoughts about her future.

"I haven't had much time to unpack or find someone to do it for me," he was saying, and Holly had to tear her gaze away from where her eyes had dropped to his button fly before he caught her ogling his package again.

Crap. Maybe she was losing her mind. Maybe this…this feeling of impending disaster was just the first sign of her unraveling mind.

Sucking in breath in an effort to calm her skittering nerves, she said, "My mother has a concierge service that could probably help." *There*, she silently congratulated herself. *That didn't sound crazy, did it?*

"Yeah? That'd be great." He thrust a hand through his hair, tousling the overlong strands even further, and she had to curl her hands into fists to stop from reaching out and smoothing the thick sun-streaked locks. "I hate unpacking," he admitted sheepishly, seemingly oblivious to her chaotic thoughts. "Even if I'd had the time, I wouldn't know where to put all this stuff. I just want my couch and TV set up so I can watch the games."

It was such a guy thing to say that she hid a smile and tried not to imagine his big body sprawled on his huge leather sofa, watching a ball game.

His body radiated clean masculine heat and where his hand touched the small of her back, as he ushered her toward the back of the house, an insidious heat spread across her flesh. She wanted to sink back into him and maybe rub against all that heat and hardness. Just as she'd done earlier.

Get a grip, woman, she ordered herself silently. *Since when did you have urges to lean on a guy for support?*

"I'll…um…call my mother in the morning." Her voice emerged low and slightly husky and she ignored the little smile teasing the corner of his mouth that she was tempted to bite right off.

She rolled her eyes. Clearly she needed food fast or she'd start nibbling on the closest patch of masculine skin.

Looking around his sparkling, modern kitchen, Holly discovered a mild case of kitchen envy but then he started pulling things out of his refrigerator with quick efficiency and she discovered another kind of envy too. The kind where she could wield a corkscrew or maybe a spatula with the same skill she handled a scalpel.

Gabriel Alexander—*the jerk*—didn't seem to suffer from the same challenges. He drew a bottle of white wine out of the cooler and efficiently uncorked it while he directed her to an overhead cabinet for wine glasses.

"I usually prefer beer," he said. "But good food demands a good wine."

She handed him the glasses. "You're a foodie?"

His eyes crinkled at the corners at her disgruntled tone. "You sound surprised."

She sighed, propped her hip against the nearest cabinet

and folded her arms beneath her breasts. "Not so much surprised as envious," she admitted. "I'm a kitchen klutz." His
lips twitched and she narrowed her eyes to dangerous slits
because she knew what he was thinking. He was thinking
the kitchen wasn't the only place she suffered from klut-
ziness.

He clearly valued his life because he just chuckled and
handed her a glass of chilled white wine. "You're a cute
klutz, though." Then he stunned her speechless by tracing
a line of fire across her lips with his finger before turning
away to reach for a bowl and a carton of eggs.

It took her a few moments—okay, minutes—to recover
her breath and gulp down a mouthful of crisp Riesling. It
jolted her back to reality before warming up her belly and
clearing her head.

She offered to chop something but he shook his head
and said he was off duty. She didn't know whether to be relieved or offended since he'd probably meant that he'd seen
enough blood for one day. *Smartass.*

So Holly sipped her wine and watched him work, which,
God knew, wasn't a hardship. It was also kind of hot to see
a man so at home in a kitchen.

When she was stressed she liked to bake but her efforts
were mostly inedible, which sucked because she loved choc-
olate-fudge brownies and chocolate-chip cookies. Granted,
she made an excellent salad but she was ashamed to say
she often just nuked one of the casseroles her mother kept
stocked in the freezer for her. It was easier than cleaning
up after her disasters.

She licked a drop of wine off the back of her hand, impressed by his one-handed method of cracking eggs into a
bowl without adding a ton of shells. S*how-off.* He then went
on to chop and sprinkle with quick efficiency until delicious
smells filled the kitchen and her stomach set up an almost
continuous growl.

Over another glass of wine and light, fluffy harvest omelets that he'd teamed with herbed bruschetta, Gabriel entertained her with stories of his youthful exploits. Holly found herself laughing more than she had in years and soon a warm glow radiated out from the center of her chest. She was flushed and light-headed—like she'd drunk too much champagne or maybe sucked on a little too much helium—and she could scarcely believe that she was sitting in a kitchen with the Hollywood Hatchet Man, actually enjoying herself.

Before she could remind herself that he'd seen countless beautiful and famous women—including her sister—naked or that he'd worked in an industry that was mostly to blame for the low self-esteem of ordinary women like herself, Holly swirled the wine in her glass and looked up, only to become snared by the sleepy heat in his eyes. *Yikes.*

"So what about you?" he asked.

Her laughter died and a palpable tension replaced the friendly mood—a tension that had absolutely nothing to do with her opinions of his former career. She blinked.

It didn't take a genius to know what he was thinking. It was there in the glowing heat of his gaze that set her pulse skittering even as a heavy ache settled between her thighs.

It might have been the wine, knocked back on an empty stomach, but her tongue felt suddenly too thick to form words. And like the night she'd slugged back mojitos, her lips went numb.

For long moments she stared into his eyes, hypnotized, until the thickening tension made it difficult to breathe. She blinked. "I…uh…"

Her voice came to her through a long tunnel and the breathless huskiness of it might have shocked her if she'd been thinking clearly…okay, thinking, period. But for the same reason her mouth couldn't form words, her brain couldn't form thoughts.

In slow motion she licked her dry lips and his gaze dropped to catch the path of her tongue. His eyes darkened and he said her name. "Holly." Just her name, but his voice, rough and deep as sin, scraped her already ragged nerves and she had to gulp in air or pass out.

Her skin gave a warning prickle an instant before her brain melted along with the muscles in her thighs.

"Hmm?" She was in big trouble and for some reason she couldn't seem to drum up the energy to care.

His eyes dipped to half-mast and she could practically feel the enormous control he was exercising over himself. It was there in the tight lines of his face and the sudden still-ness of his body, which practically vibrated with tension.

And there was absolutely no mistaking the sensuality in his gaze.

"If you're going to leave," he rasped in a voice she scarcely recognized, "I suggest you do it now."

Feeling dazed and strangely lethargic, Holly sucked in a shuddery breath. "Um…now?" Frankly, she didn't know how he expected her to move. She was frozen to the spot by the laser-bright gaze, the gold flecks swirling in the blue-green depths having stolen her ability to move.

"I'm giving you ten seconds." The warning came as a low deep growl that sent a dark excitement skittering through her blood until her body was practically humming with anticipation.

His gaze darkened—"Nine"—and her pulse gave an ex-cited little blip. Instead of scrambling to her feet and escap-ing, she continued staring into his eyes, wondering at this odd dark need to ride the edge of danger.

A voice in her head ordered her to move, but her body refused to obey. "And then what?"

He leaned forward until there was barely an inch sep-arating his lips from hers. Fascinated, she stared into the swirling depths of his eyes and was stunned by the inten-sity burning in their centers. He appeared seconds away from pouncing and a thrill of alarm zinged across her skin.

Dropping her gaze, she found his finely sculpted mouth

almost touching hers. *Oh, God.* He was so close she could already feel the searing imprint of his mouth. She eagerly awaited a kiss she knew was just a heartbeat away.

And when he didn't so much as lean in her direction she was the one to make the move that closed the gap between their mouths. Through the roaring in her head she thought she heard him say, "And then I'm going to drag you over the counter and there'll be no escaping until—"

She froze. "Until?"

She felt him smile against her lips and the sensation of it sent a firestorm of sparks exploding in her brain like fireworks. "Until your eyes roll back in your head and..." Her breath escaped in a shuddery whoosh. "And you forget your plan."

She wondered why he was still talking when all she wanted was for him to grab her and make her eyes roll back in her head. Oh, wait. They'd already rolled back in her head to check out the state of her brain and "My plan? What plan?" popped out of her mouth in a breathless rush. It took a few seconds for her words to finally register. And when they did, her head cleared.

"Oh." She abruptly shoved back from the counter, nearly toppling the stool in her haste. For a breathless moment she stood, swaying, and stared at him with wide, panicked eyes. "I...um, I have to go."

Gabriel made a growling sound deep in his chest that had the hair on her arms lifting like she'd got too close to an electrostatic generator. Spooked by the sensations and the thoughts racing through her head, Holly backed away, turned on her heel and walked blindly into the wall.

"Careful," he murmured, and even without looking she knew he was fighting a smile. She rolled her eyes and altered her course, heading down the passage to the front of the house, suddenly eager to escape. Before she did something she regretted.

Like turn and grab him. Like lose herself in his hungry

caresses or forget that she had a plan that had no room for hot, sexy surgeons.

"I have to go," she repeated, feeling a little dazed and more than a little freaked out. Her ears buzzed and her knees shook so badly it was a miracle they didn't buckle and dump her on her ass.

"I'll see you home." His voice came from right behind her and a wide-eyed look over her shoulder revealed him fighting amusement. *Oh, God, how embarrassing.* She increased her pace until the urgent tap-tap of her heels on the wooden floorboards nearly drowned out her panicked thoughts.

"There's no need," she babbled, as she finally reached the door and tried to tug it open, only to find it locked. "Besides, I'm right next…door and—" emerged on a breathless squeak when she swung around to find him only inches away.

Gabriel regarded her silently for an endless moment before he scooped up her shoulder bag and briefcase. She held out a shaking hand. "I'll see you home," he repeated in a gravelly voice, and reached around her to open the door.

She might have escaped unscathed if she hadn't made the mistake of lifting her gaze off his white T-shirt-covered chest, up past his tanned throat, the hard square jaw and sculpted mouth to his gaze.

She froze.

His pupils were huge and very black, his eyes hot and steamy in his tanned face. More blue than green, they blazed with an emotion that was unmistakable even to a social klutz like her.

For long charged moments their gazes locked until with a savage growl Gabriel kicked the door closed and hauled Holly up against him. And before she could squeak out a protest at the rough treatment, he'd backed her against the door and closed his mouth over hers in a kiss so hot it singed her skin and set her hair on fire.

Ohmigod.

Incredible heat poured off him in waves that engulfed

her, threatening to drag her under and drown her in a flood of heat and urgency. *Help,* she thought an instant before his tongue breached the barrier of her lips, surging into her mouth and stealing her breath. *I'm in trouble.*

His tongue slid against hers and the next instant the kiss turned greedy, his mouth eating hungrily at hers. She moaned and desperation rose along with the heat in his kisses. Any thought of escaping faded.

In fact, if this was trouble she welcomed it, along with the slick slide of his tongue against hers and the warm press of his big hard body.

Fever rose in her blood and her skin prickled with an almost embarrassing need to be touched, a need for his big warm hands to slide over her naked flesh.

He broke off the kiss to feather his lips across her jaw to the delicate skin beneath her ear, leaving Holly fighting for breath and the urge to beg him to hurry. Heat exploded along her nerve endings and she shuddered, her breasts tightening until they ached.

She flattened her palms against his belly; the bunching muscles making her hands itch with the need to explore every hard inch of him, including the long thick evidence of his arousal against her belly.

Unable to resist arching closer, Holly angled her head and "Gabriel...I...um..." emerged on a low moan. She wasn't sure what she'd meant to say, only that a voice, somewhere in the far reaches of her mind, was urging her to get the hell away before it was too late. "I have to...I need to I think I should..."

"Don't," he murmured against her throat, and she murmured in dazed agreement. "Don't think." Nipping at the slender column, he drew her skin into his mouth, soothing the small hurt when she uttered a tiny shocked gasp. "Feel, Holly. Just...feel."

Okay, so that was doable. Besides, thinking took too much effort, especially with his mouth, hot and wet as it dragged across her skin, making secret hidden flesh respond with tiny spasmodic clenches.

She stiffened. *Oh, God.* He'd yanked her right to the edge so fast she was fighting to keep from exploding right out of her skin.

Then he was taking her mouth again in a hungry kiss, thrusting a hard thigh between hers and pressing his erection into the notch at the top of her thighs. His big hands slid to her hips, his fingers sinking into her soft flesh as he ground against her, groaning like he was in pain. And before she could give voice to the fiery need clawing at her belly, his muscles bunched and she found herself lifted off her feet.

Instinctively wrapping her legs around his hips, Holly clutched at his shoulders. Muscles shifted beneath her hands, a solid anchor in a world suddenly whirling with chaotic hunger, ragged breathing and wild exhilaration.

Her hair, a dark silky nimbus, floated around their heads. Somehow he'd unraveled her hair with the same ease that he'd unraveled her defenses.

"Hold on," he said, pushing away from the door to stand swaying for a couple of beats, breath sawing from his heaving lungs like he'd crossed the Brooklyn Bridge at a dead run.

"Wha-at?" Holly's lashes fluttered up and she stared at him uncomprehendingly. Without replying, he turned toward the sitting room, cursing when his foot caught on something and he staggered. She squeaked and tightened her grip and his muttered curse of "Damn boxes" became a soothing growl. "Don't worry," he murmured against her mouth between kisses. "I won't let you fall."

CHAPTER EIGHT

HOLLY HAD A brief thought that it was too late for that. Way too late to prevent her heart from getting bruised by a man as handsome and flawless as his celestial namesake.

Then a couple feet beyond the door his knees connected with something solid and the next instant she found herself literally falling. She sucked in a startled breath, tightened her grip, and before she could squeak out a protest she was on her back with Gabe's big body sprawled over the top of hers.

"Oomph."

"Sorry," he breathed beside her ear. "You're heavier than I expected."

"Or maybe," she retorted, unable to prevent the pleased grin from forming when she turned her head to give his earlobe a punishing nip and a groan accompanied the shudder moving through him, "you're not as manly as you think."

His response was an explosive snort that questioned her sanity.

"Oh, yeah?" he breathed, his teeth flashing white in the near darkness as he levered himself onto his elbows. The move pressed his hips closer, setting off an explosion of starbursts behind her eyes. "I'll show you manly."

She groaned, as much at the typically macho statement as the feel of him, long and thick and incredibly hard as he pressed tightly against her crotch. Suspended in sensation and every nerve ending firing simultaneously, it was more than she could handle. More than she could ever remember feeling. And just as a glimmer of panic threatened to break free of the haze of need and greed clouding her brain, Gabriel smoothed a hand from her bottom down the long length of her femur to her knee and back again.

"God, you have no idea how much I want you," he murmured, leaning forward to run his tongue from the corner of her mouth to the sweet spot beneath her ear.

But Holly did, and in response her core melted and clenched in anticipation.

He rose up onto his knees with a low, thrilling growl and reached for the back of his T-shirt, yanking it over his head in one smooth move that left Holly speechless. And not just from the speed of his actions.

His torso was a marvel of masculine perfection that she couldn't help but reach out and touch. She wanted to see him. Wanted to explore his physical perfection with her hands and her mouth.

Unable to stop herself, she slid her hands over his skin, reveling in the tanned skin, taut and smooth across his hard, ridged flesh. His skin was slightly damp beneath her questing fingers as muscles bunched and rippled at her touch.

Light spilled from the foyer, surrounding his darkened form like a full-body halo, and the image of a golden angel, fallen to earth to tempt mortal women to sin, returned. And, *darn it*, she was more than ready to become one of the fallen right alongside.

He was a beautiful man and for a blinding moment of panic she wondered what he was doing with her—what he would say when he saw the rest of her scars, especially the ugly one marring the length of her thigh. But then he fumbled, his hands shaking in his haste to undress, and she realized that she'd made him tremble. Her touch had made him shake like a boy.

It was a little overwhelming.

Then he was unbuttoning his fly. Her eyes widened along with every inch that became exposed and suddenly over-whelming was nothing compared to the sight of him.

"Wha-what are you doing?"

He looked up, his teeth gleaming in the near darkness. He took in her wide-eyed expression and rasped out an in-credulous laugh. "Well, Doc," he managed roughly. "This is what's called getting naked. It's what happens before a man pulls out—"

Holly squeaked and slapped her hands over her ears in a move that belied her professional status. Gabriel's eyebrows almost disappeared into his hairline and he leaned forward to pull one of her hands free. "I was going to say protection, Dr. Buchanan," he finished dryly.

She gulped and fought the blush heating her face. "But… but we're in the sitting room."

He sent an indifferent glance across his shoulder at the huge bay window before turning back to renew his button attack. "I can't wait," he growled, lifting her up so he could strip off her jacket.

Her breath hitched at the impatience in his voice, his every jerky movement, and felt her core quiver in anticipa-tion of the big event. "But…the curtains."

"No one can see you." He shoved the jeans down his legs and kicked them aside, settling back to study the lacy shell molded to her curves. "Besides, it's dark."

Not that dark, Holly thought. *You'll see me*. And, oh, boy, she could see him too.

"That's the point," he murmured in a voice as rough and deep as sin, telling her she'd spoken her thoughts out loud. "I can't wait to get you all the way naked so I can see you."

That's exactly what she didn't want.

"All of you, Holly." He dropped his hands to the hem of her shell, his fingers brushing the bare flesh of her belly. It quivered. "And then," he promised in a wicked whisper,

"I'm going to take you upstairs and I'm going to start all… over…again."

Her splutter of surprise ended on a gasp when he whipped her shell over her head and dropped it on the floor beside the sofa. She tried to shield herself from his gaze but he grabbed her wrists to prevent her from hiding.

Finally his eyes lifted and locked on hers. Holly sucked in a sharp breath as heat rose up her neck into her face along with the heat heading for her core. "Gabriel," she whispered beseechingly, but he leaned forward to trace a shaking finger across the tops of her breasts, interrupting her with a growl of appreciation when her nipples peaked.

"Don't hide, Holly."

She turned her face away. "You're…um…staring."

His chuckle was a deep velvet slide across her senses that made her quiver. "God, yes," he drawled. "You're so damn beautiful." And then quietly, as though he was talking to himself, he murmured, "More beautiful than I remember."

Her mouth dropped open and for a moment she wondered if he was hallucinating or drunk. Her words rushed out on a rising squeak of outrage. "You saw me naked? Wh-when?"

His hands soothed a fiery path up her arms to her shoulders where he slid his fingers beneath the lacy straps of her bra. "That black swimsuit doesn't hide a damn thing." He grinned, tugging them down over her shoulders.

Her mouth open and closed a couple times and he shook his head, although Holly wasn't sure what it meant.

"My plan…" she began breathlessly, but he leaned down and gave her a hard kiss.

"Will still be there tomorrow."

"Well, okay, then…" she murmured against his mouth. "I guess just this once…won't…um…hurt. Will it?"

"No." His voice shook with laughter. "I promise it won't hurt." Then his hands slid back over her shoulders. His knuckles brushed her collarbone as he moved to the tops of her breasts. It was difficult to read his expression.

Heck. It was difficult to think.

Then she stopped caring because his sensual mouth slid to her throat and his hand slid beneath the layer of stretchy lace to cup her bare breast. Her shocked breath was loud in the heavy silence and shudders of pleasure leapt and grew at the feel of his warm calloused hand cupping and squeezing her gently, his thumb scraping a line of fire across her flesh.

Her nipples tightened into hard points and she couldn't prevent a moan from escaping at the exquisite pain. Her back arched, the move pushing her breast into his warm, rough palm. Her hands moved across his shoulders, up his neck to fist his warm silky hair, pulling him closer...closer to where his mouth could close over her nipple and soothe the terrible ache he'd created.

If she'd been thinking she might have been horrified by her wanton behavior, but she wasn't...couldn't...because within seconds Gabriel had stripped her naked and the sound he uttered, a mix of pain and strangled laughter that came from deep in his chest, made her ache. And thrill. *God, what a thrill!*

Before she could get self-conscious or beg him to press his naked body to hers, he leaned down and placed a soft kiss on each breast. She trembled at the tenderness of the gesture and when he drew one peak into his mouth, his tongue sliding across her nipple, hot and wet and relentless, a ragged moan tore loose from deep in her throat.

He lifted his head. "Your heart is pounding." She blinked up into his face but his expression was hidden in shadow and she couldn't tell what he was thinking.

"What?"

His eyes were dark and fathomless. "Tell me you want me."

Oh, God. "Wha-a-at?"

"Say it and I'll give you what you need."

Holly sucked in a breath. "I...I..." For some reason she couldn't get the words past the hot lump of need in her throat. He lowered his head and gave her nipple a tiny punishing nip and the words finally escaped on a rush of air. "Ohmigodiwantyou."

And then, tired of waiting, Holly reached up and with hands fisted in his soft hair brought his mouth down to hers so she could kiss him, reveling in the ragged groan wrenched from deep within his chest. She loved the way he kissed; like he was starving for the taste of her. She was starving for the taste of him too and the kiss became an avaricious frenzy of mouths and tongues and grasping hands. And when Gabe shifted and thrust into her, Holly arched her back and begged for more.

Holly begged for more and Gabriel gave her more. More kisses, more climaxes and more…everything. He'd given her more than he'd given any woman in a long time. Maybe ever. And when it was over and she lay in a boneless heap across his chest, Gabe wondered what the hell had happened.

What had started out as simply satisfying a physical need had taken on a life of its own until he'd felt a desperation to take her someplace she'd never been. The only thing was— he'd been taken there too. And he wasn't entirely comfortable with the discovery.

They were both damp with exertion and his thundering pulse almost drowned out the sound of her ragged breathing.

Or was that his ragged breathing?

He felt completely wrung out and too lethargic to move them somewhere more comfortable. Like his bed.

He had plans for Holly and his bed.

After a few minutes, he groaned and lifted a large hand to soothe a line from her shoulder, down her back to her bottom. She was soft and silky and so touchable he couldn't resist repeating the move until she murmured in the back of her throat and shifted against him, so slowly and sinuously that he went instantly hard.

"Someone stole my bones while we were busy," he murmured sleepily, smiling when she grunted softly against his skin.

"Are you sure? I think I feel at least one they left behind," she murmured, her breath tickling his chest and sending arrows of heat into his groin, hardening his erection and fueling his hunger. "If they hadn't also stolen mine I'd help you find it."

She sighed sleepily and nuzzled closer. He slid his arms around her and nudged her closer, burying his face in her wild hair and breathing in her unique scent. It was warm and fresh with a hint of something elusive. Kind of like the woman herself.

Realizing he was breathing in a woman like she was his air, Gabe stilled. He'd never been a nuzzler. Or a cuddler, for that matter. He was usually looking for his clothes by now, ready to make his escape. But he didn't want to escape. In fact, he wanted to find the source of that scent and was prepared to spend the rest of the night searching for it.

He'd thought once would be enough. He'd rock her world, walk her home and go back to getting his life on track. *Hell.* Hadn't she been the one to put a limit on this?

And he'd been okay with that. Surprisingly, only a few minutes had passed since he'd climaxed but he was already gearing up for round two.

Clearly he wasn't done with her yet.

"Damn New York thieves."

Her mouth curved against his skin. "What makes you certain they were from New York? Maybe they followed you from California."

"Yeah, and maybe you need to move your knee before you cut off my blood supply."

She snickered and gently shifted her knee until he swore he saw stars. He grunted and grabbed her thigh to halt her movement. She said, "Oops, sorry," in a voice that didn't sound very sincere. "Guess I found that bone." Then she yawned and stretched all those silky curves against him and the stars became firebursts of renewed lust.

"I guess it's also time to go," she murmured sleepily. "Make me go, Gabriel."

He didn't like the idea of her leaving. "Not yet," he said, wrapping his arms around her and heaving up off the couch where he stood swaying for a few beats while he waited for blood to reach his brain. "Later."

Much later.

Holly didn't know how she'd ended up in Gabe's bed. He'd hauled her into the shower, soaped every inch of her and then ensured she'd been completely soap-free with his hands and mouth. And when she'd been a boneless lump he'd wrapped her up in a huge towel and lifted her in his arms.

"And now," he growled in a voice as deep and rough as if he'd just awakened from a night of sin, "I'm taking you to bed."

The thought of getting to explore his big body sent tingles of anticipation racing over Holly's flesh. They'd been too desperate earlier to do more than race for the finish and Holly wanted to explore his big, brawny body with more than her hands. She wanted to use her mouth and tongue and eyes to explore every last inch of him. Her mouth watered.

Oh, and she wanted to discover the rest of him too.

He tossed her roughly on the bed, following her down to nip her shoulder lightly, chuckling when goose-bumps raced over her damp skin. Instead of ravishing her, like she'd thought—okay, hoped—he stretched across her body to pull out an unopened box of condoms from the bedside table.

"I thought you said you didn't have any," she said a little breathlessly, and reached out to untie the towel hiding his goodies from her.

Gabriel snorted out a laugh. "I lied."

"Some Boy Scout you are."

"I lied about that too," he admitted, straddling her body

and unwrapping her like she was an unexpected gift he'd found on his pillow. "I was too busy impressing the girls with my awesome skills." He chuckled at her expression and leaned forward to plant a lightning fast kiss on her mouth. "I meant in surfing." He fumbled with the box. "Damn it," he snarled, "I can't open this thing."

By this time he was panting and swearing and when Holly tried to help, the box popped open and silver squares flew everywhere. Gabe simply snatched one, planted a big hand in the middle of her chest and shoved her backwards. Holly gave a breathless laugh and before she could tell him to hurry, he'd covered himself and was sliding between her legs.

"Now, Dr. Buchanan," he growled, "I'm going to rock your world. Again."

Holly's skeptical snort ended on a long, low moan as he thrust into her, her body stretching deliciously as it accommodated his size.

Oh, God, he totally had, was her last conscious thought. *He'd totally rocked her world.*

Holly jerked awake with no idea of the time or where she was. One thing she did know was that something heavy pinned her to the bed. Something heavy, slightly hairy and toasty warm.

She frowned sleepily and stretched, wondering at the slight ache in her muscles. Like she'd spent the night in... rigorous...exercise... *Oh...my...God*, she thought, sucking in a sharp breath as recollection returned in a rush of heat and embarrassment and...and... *What the heck have I done?*

For several long seconds she lay there, not breathing, until a firm voice in the back of her head told her to get her butt into gear.

Exhaling shakily, she took stock of the situation and tried not to panic. But despite the overwhelming urge to jump up and run screaming from Gabriel's house, she couldn't help noticing the large body surrounding her like a living blanket.

Fine. So one would think that she'd noticed enough of that big, muscular body in the hours they'd spent… Yes, well, she wasn't going to think about that now. If she did she might lose it or…or jump his bones…again.

Kind of like she'd done in the deep, dark hours of the night.

Her face flamed. And when something else flamed deep in her belly, it galvanized her into action.

Holding her breath, she carefully slid out from beneath his sprawling body and felt cool air brush her exposed skin. She shivered. It was touch and go there for a while when every strand of DNA urged her to slide back against the heated furnace while instinct told her to get the heck out of Dodge.

Besides, they'd agreed. One time only. So maybe it had stretched to two and then three…*gulp*…but it was still one night.

Right? Her breath escaped in long whoosh. Right.

She made the mistake of looking over her shoulder at him and got stuck on the stark beauty of his long swimmer's body, sprawled face-down across the huge bed and illuminated by the light spilling from the bathroom. His back was a marvel of masculine perfection, the wide, powerful shoulders tapering to narrow hips, a tight butt—with those sexy little scoops at the sides—and long muscular legs ending in large brawny feet.

For one yearning moment she fought against the desire to reach out and touch but then he grunted and shifted as though he missed her already—boy, she could identify—and the instinct to flee returned.

Stifling a little squeak of panic, Holly slid off the bed and headed for the door. Her clothes were still downstairs—scattered all over his sitting room. *Yikes.*

She paused at the bedroom door, wondering if she should

wake him, but the thought of facing him after everything they'd done was just too disturbing. And considering where he'd had his mouth not too long ago—okay, and where she'd had hers—the last thing she needed was looking into his blue-green gaze and seeing knowledge and…awareness.

She'd rather run through the streets naked. Something she might have to do if she couldn't find her damn clothes.

Turning, she hobbled down the stairs in the dark, wondering where the heck all these aching muscles had come from. She stubbed her toe on her way into the sitting room and hopped on one foot as she hunted around for her clothes, pulling on items as she found them.

After a fruitless search for her underwear, she huffed out an impatient breath and swiftly buttoned her jacket over her unbound breasts. *Damn it.* She felt like everyone would know it too but the longer she lingered, the more chance there was of Gabriel waking and— And that was the absolute last thing she wanted.

So she'd have to ditch her underwear. Darn. And it was new too.

She knew she'd have to face Gabriel sometime but as for right this minute? No way in hell was she sticking around to find her panties and bra. Besides, glossing over someone's scars while in the grip of a desperate hunger was one thing, looking into his eyes in the cold aftermath of a hot night was something else entirely.

No. Not gonna happen. She'd rather lose her underwear and hope they'd disappeared altogether. Poof. Into thin air.

Grabbing her strappy heels, she headed into the foyer, where he'd dropped her briefcase and shoulder bag what seemed like days ago rather than a few short hours. Then with a quick guilty glance over her shoulder she quietly let herself out of the house.

Her one night of screaming exercise was over.

Time to get back on track.

It took her less than a minute to hightail it to her own

front door, all the while looking around guiltily and wishing she didn't feel like an errant adolescent sneaking in after curfew.

She let herself in and quietly thunked her forehead against the door a couple times, her breath escaping in a whoosh of relief and for some reason fighting the urge to cry. Damn it, what the heck was wrong with—?

"Long night?"

Holly gave a startled squeak and whirled so fast she nearly fell over. She backed against the door to give her shaky knees much-needed support and stared wide-eyed at Sam, slouched casually in the sitting-room doorway, watching her over the top of his mug.

He was dressed in a pair of unbuttoned jeans…and nothing else. Just a few months ago the sight of his sculpted chest would have sent her heart racing and her tongue swelling in her throat. But now all she wanted to do was run and hide and maybe freak out, because she'd seen Gabriel Alexander's awesome body and no one else could compare.

Sam's dark eyes took in her rumpled appearance and his expression turned wry. "Ah," he drawled, and lifted his mug in a silent toast.

Holly didn't need any interpretation of the brief flash of amusement but she opened her mouth and "What?" popped out before she could stop it.

"Really?" he murmured, his eyes going unerringly to her mouth then dropping to her neck before lifting to lock gazes with her. Beneath the humor was understanding. "You want to go there?"

Holly assumed an innocent expression. "I don't know what you're talking about."

"You bailed, Buchanan."

Guilt flashed like a neon light behind her eyes.

"I…uh…pfft… No."

"It's okay, Holly," he interrupted quietly, his eyes going oddly flat. "We've all done it." And then without another word he turned and disappeared, leaving Holly battling curiosity, embarrassment and a desire to go pull the covers over her head and hope that when she woke she'd find it had all been a horrible dream.

An image flashed into her head of Gabriel's expression as he rose over her and she got a full-body flush and shiver all at once.

Okay. Maybe not so horrible.

CHAPTER NINE

LIGHT STREAMED IN through the cracks in the curtain and fell across Gabe's face. He groaned and tried to lift his head but he felt like someone had run over him with a compacting roller—the ones they used on golfing greens—leaving him flattened.

Almost immediately he realized what had woken him. Firstly, his pager and his cellphone were both buzzing angrily in his ear, and secondly…his bed was cool and empty.

The buzzing was an annoying reminder that he needed to get to the hospital, but the latter…hell, he didn't know what to think. Only that he wasn't happy that she'd left without waking him—especially with the smell of her still clinging to his pillow and sheets.

He turned and sniffed his shoulder.

And his skin, damn it.

Rolling over, he grabbed his phone and told himself it was a good thing because now he wouldn't have to deal with any morning-after expectations. He just hadn't pegged Holly for the hit-and-run type. But what did he really know about her other than she wore class and refinement like a shield, and that she hated being stared at?

She was just another woman, he reminded himself, and he'd learned a long time ago that he wasn't cut out for more than a good time. It was coded into his genes.

Besides, she'd been the one to say this was a one-time thing and one-time things were his specialty.

He growled, "Yeah?" into the phone and listened to the nurse on the other end then ended the call. Then he rolled off the bed and headed for the bathroom. His day promised to be a whirlwind of surgeries and meetings, and with the information the nurse had just given him, he might just have to alter his schedule.

He arrived in ICU just as Holly was leaving. Her stride faltered when she saw him but even though she greeted him, she avoided his gaze. If he hadn't seen the wild tide of color surging beneath her creamy skin he might have thought she'd forgotten his existence the instant she'd walked out his front door.

But it was the sight of her, once again coolly elegant, that made him want to push her up against the wall and mess her up a little. Starting with her hair, which was pulled into a neat French twist.

She hadn't seemed to mind so much last night, he told himself, recalling with perfect clarity the dark, silky curtain framing her face and brushing against his skin as she'd memorized every inch of his body with her mouth.

Just that fast he was hard—harder than he'd been last night. Harder than he'd ever been, because now he knew that beneath the prim little suits and cool, professional mask was an incredibly enthusiastic woman eager to give as much as she received.

"Holly—" he began.

But she interrupted him with a hasty "Excuse me, Dr. Alexander, but I'm needed in surgery," leaving him gaping at her straight spine and swaying hips as she disappeared down the passage with an urgent tap, tap, tap of those sexy slingbacks.

What the—?

"Dr. Alexander?"

Gabe turned to see the head of ICU pop her head out the door. "Yeah?"

"We need you."

Yeah, well. Looks like you're the only one.

He sighed and shoved a hand through his hair, wondering if he'd lost his mind. Here he was, standing staring after a woman who'd made it abundantly clear that he was a one-time deal and… *Hell.* He shoved a hand through his hair again and blew out a frustrated breath. What the heck did he think he was going to do when…*if*…he caught up with her? Grab her? Push her up against the wall and kiss her until she moaned and looked at him through dazed, smoky eyes?

Jeez.

"I'm all yours," he sighed.

And chuckled when the older woman pretended to swoon and muttered a heartfelt "If only," before disappearing back into ICU.

Yeah, he thought dryly. If only. If only his one-night stand hadn't managed to rock his world. Three times.

Realizing he was standing around, obsessing about a woman who wasn't interested in a repeat, Gabe scowled and shoved through the doors, wondering when the hell he'd turned into such a damn girl.

Holly practically ran from ICU as if the paparazzi were in pursuit after an anonymous tip-off. Her skin burned with the mortification of having to face him so soon after…well, so soon. Because, frankly? She'd like to forget last night had ever happened.

Good luck with that.

"Oh, be quiet," she snarled to the annoying snicker in her head, startling a couple of nurses passing her in the hallway. They gave her strange looks but Holly was accustomed to people staring so she ignored them and headed for the nearest bathroom.

Once she made sure she was alone, she headed for the

basins and flipped on the cold water. Breathing like she'd stepped out and found herself at five thousand feet, she splashed her face until her ears stopped ringing and she didn't feel like her head was about to pop off her shoulders.

She made the mistake of looking into the mirror and nearly gave herself a stroke when she encountered her smoky, heavy-lidded gaze. *Ohmigod, I look like I just got lucky.*

A low sound emerged from her throat that sounded too much like a whimper for Holly's peace of mind. Her gaze dropped unerringly to her bruised, swollen lips and she recalled with absolute clarity the way Gabriel kissed. He'd consumed her like she was a rare delicacy he was determined to savor…as if his very life depended on it. A shiver of remembered delight skated up her spine. As if that light suction was an invitation to surrender, her soul along with her body.

Realizing she was hyperventilating, Holly splashed herself again. She didn't think she could walk out of this bathroom and not have people look at her without them knowing exactly what she'd been up to.

Groaning, she grabbed a wad of paper towels from the dispenser just as the door opened. Hoping it wasn't anyone she knew, Holly began patting her face dry.

"Holly?"

She froze. Oh, God. It had to be Tess, didn't it? Tess would see at a glance that she was a total mess.

"Are you okay?"

Sucking in a steadying breath, Holly met her gaze in the mirror, casually patting her skin dry. "Sure," she croaked. "Why?"

Tess moved closer. "Kimberlyn said she saw you tear out of the house this morning as though your underwear was on fire. Did something happen?"

At the mention of her underwear, Holly gave a strangled gurgle that she tried to cover up by coughing. Had something happened? Where to start? Forget that her underwear had practically caught fire—which was why it was currently gracing Gabriel's sitting room. Somewhere.

"No." Not going there.

The next instant Tessa was whipping her around, her eyes concerned as she took in Holly's expression.

"Oh, honey, what's wrong?" she urged. "It is your mother? Father?" Her concern abruptly turned to a gasp when she caught sight of Holly's neck. *"Ohmigod."* Her eyes widened with shock. "You've got a…*hickey*?"

"No! Jeez." Holly slapped a hand over the offending mark she'd discovered this morning—along with at least three others in embarrassing places—when she'd stripped in the bathroom, intending to wash away every trace of the night.

"It is." Tessa looked absolutely delighted by the sight. "It so is a hickey." She grabbed Holly's hand. "Let me see."

Holly squeaked and slapped her free hand over the mark. "Damn it, Tess." She covered her flaming face with her free hand and groaned. "What are we, in high school?"

"Oh, come on." Tessa spluttered with laughter. "Let the pregnant woman have her way or she'll get all hormonal on your ass." Then seeing the embarrassed misery on Holly's face she froze, her eyes going soft and concerned again.

"Oh, honey, why the long face? It's supposed to relax you, not make you tense enough to shatter."

Holly ignored her statement because she felt as though one wrong move and she'd— "I didn't mean for it to happen," she wailed helplessly as she pulled at her collar and turned to study the mark on her neck. There was another high on the inside of her thigh, one in the crease separating her hip and thigh and one—fine, two—on her breasts.

She blushed.

"Did the bastard say something about your scars?" Tessa demanded. "I hope you punched his—"

"N-no-o." Holly spluttered out a strangled laugh. "He didn't. He really didn't," she repeated, recalling exactly what he done to every single one of the blemishes marring her skin. With his lips and tongue.

Tessa's gaze turned sympathetic. "Oh, God, it was awful. Is that it?"

"Will you just stop?" Holly spluttered out on a mortified laugh. "No, it wasn't awful, it was…um…fine." By this time she wanted to climb into the basin and drown herself. Instead, she opened the faucet again, this time burying her burning face in her water-filled cupped hands, hoping Tess would just go away.

So, okay, it had been more than fine. Try spectacular. Amazing. Incredible.

And it was over.

Tessa was still there to hand over a wad of paper towels. Holly muttered her thanks and sent her friend a narrow-eyed sideways glance when her mouth twitched. Tessa quickly lifted a hand to hide her smile.

"Okay, so it was…*fine*," her friend said agreeably, but her voice wobbled as though she was fighting laughter. "Then why are you so…um…upset?"

Holly sucked in a breath and—*thank God*—was saved from replying by a sudden beeping. Whipping out her pager, she glanced at the screen. "I've got to go," she said apologetically, hugely relieved because she had absolutely no idea why she was freaking out and even less idea of how to explain it.

She dropped the wadded paper towels into the trash and headed for the door, yanking it open so fast she nearly bopped herself on the nose.

"I want details, Dr. Buchanan," Tessa called out, and a horrified Holly sent her a you-have-got-to-be-kidding-me glance over her shoulder. She left Tessa standing in the doorway of the bathroom with a secret smile.

Holly managed to avoid Gabriel for a whole week. And it wasn't easy. First, by being so busy she barely had time to think, and, second, by peeping out the bay window to see if the coast was clear before bolting from the house.

The nights? Well, she hadn't been so lucky there. Now that she knew where Gabriel's bedroom was located she realized they shared a wall. A wall that gave her endless nightmares—okay, sleepless nights—and really, *really* hot dreams that made her blush when she thought about them.

It was like her mind had…well, a mind of its own, emerging at night to torment her with images she was able to control during the day. Fine. Mostly control.

Besides, she'd known him, what…six weeks? And for most of that time she'd gone out of her way to avoid him. For most of that time she'd considered him the Hollywood Hatchet Man.

"I won't let you fall," he'd said. But he'd lied. Because Holly was in danger of doing just that and there would be no one to catch her. Fortunately for her, now that she knew the danger she could protect herself by continuing to avoid him like a tax audit.

Good idea.

No problem.

No problem at all.

"How's that working out?"

Holly's head shot up. "What?" She blinked at Dr. Syu over the final stages of the tissue expansion procedure they were performing on a snakebite patient.

"You said 'No problem at all,' and attacked that scar tissue like it's a blight on the butt of humanity."

"Just thinking out loud," she lied, returning her attention to what her hands were doing. Good idea to focus on what your hands are doing, Holly, instead of thinking about "it"…*oh, God*…and him.

Holly finally completed the task of reattaching the expanded skin over the wound and was stripping off her surgical gown.

"Great job as usual, everyone," Lin Syu called as she hurried for the exit. "Holly, go home, get some rest and work out those issues you're having with yourself. The noises in your head are starting to show."

An hour later, she was heading out, exhausted and seriously considering sleeping for the next few days—which she had off.

Her mother had called that morning, inviting her home for the weekend, ostensibly to talk about the charity ball, but Holly knew Delia had other motives. Like casually introducing some unattached guy she just happened to invite—along with a bunch of other people—to her father's birthday dinner.

She planned on showing up for dinner but there was no way—no way in hell—she was getting sucked into her mother's machinations, no matter how well intentioned.

Scrolling through messages and emails that had backed up over the past few days, Holly strode through the automatic doors and barely escaped colliding with a brick wall. Her gasp turned into a muffled shriek when the wall spun around and she caught a glimpse of surprised green-blue eyes.

He must have anticipated another graceful Holly moment—which was ridiculous considering both her feet were once again firmly planted on the ground—because warm fingers wrapped around her wrist and he yanked her against him, hard enough to knock a startled "Omph" from her.

For long moments she stared at the small white button an inch from the tip of her nose and tried not to notice that she was pressed up against the very chest, belly and hard thighs—*oh, boy*—that she'd spent the past week trying not to think about.

And failing spectacularly.

After a couple of beats she lifted her gaze up his throat and square jaw, shadowed with a day's growth of stubble, to his sculpted lips, where she got caught. Her mouth watered. One corner curled with what she knew was amusement at her clumsiness and she had to seriously tear her gaze away or end up drooling like an idiot.

"Good evening, Dr. Buchanan. Fancy bumping into you," he drawled, his deep, intimate voice sending shards of longing arrowing into places that should have gone back into hibernation. Should have, darn it. But hadn't.

Lifting her gaze almost reluctantly, her breath caught at the heat burning in the blue-green depths. Heat, irony and... and an odd emotion she would have sworn was loneliness. It flashed for an instant and then was gone and she was left wondering if she'd imagined it.

Lonely? Dr. Celebrity? *Phfft!* Yeah, right. There were probably a hundred women waiting this very minute for him to turn that sexy, sleepy look their way.

Wrestling with the shocking notion, she managed a strangled "Oh" and stared up at him, wondering why it felt like her chest was being squeezed by a giant fist. Finally realizing she was holding her breath and fisting his pristine dress shirt like she was afraid she would fall at his feet if she let go, Holly unclenched her fingers one by one and slowly exhaled.

She dropped her gaze to where her hands were flattened against his chest and tried unsuccessfully to smooth the wrinkled cotton. The muscles beneath her hand hardened and the raw sound he made, low and deep in his chest, had her gaze flying upwards. His eyes turned black and he sucked in a sharp breath as if he was struggling to control some pretty powerful inclinations. Inclinations she was fighting as well.

Realizing she was stroking his chest, she gave a bleat of distress and used her flattened palms to shove away from him. Okay, so she tried to shove away, but Gabriel's arms tightened and every part of her pressed against him did a happy celebratory dance—especially the parts that could feel *his* very substantial parts...part.

She made a helpless sound that she wanted to bite back

the instant it emerged. He growled out a ragged "Holly" and her head went light and her belly clenched at the rough, raw sound.

It scraped against her jangled nerves, making her shiver. A full-body shiver he couldn't help but notice. He cleared his throat and slid a fiery visual path across her features. "You've been avoiding me." There was accusation in his tone if not in his eyes—which were soaking her up like a sponge.

Guilt sneaked up on her and she blurted out, "Wha—? No...I—" His permanently arched brow rose up his forehead, the very move chiding her blatant lie. "It's just that... I...um." She broke off on a ragged breath and cast around in panic for a believable excuse. But she'd never been particularly good at lying. "It was a one-time thing," she reminded him weakly. "I just thought it would be easier if we didn't...I mean... Oh, God...help me out here."

"Have dinner with me."

The quiet request—that seemed not so much a request as a command—startled her. She cautiously eased herself out of his arms and drew in a lungful of air that smelled only faintly of him. *Thank God.* Plastered up against him, all she'd been able to smell had been something dark and masculine. Something that had hit her brain like a blast of pheromones and had made her sway dizzily, and when he reached out to steady her, she backed up like a startled deer.

She lifted a hand to her spinning head. "Dinner?"

Looking somewhat baffled by her behavior, he shoved his hands into his trouser pockets and stared at her, his normally wicked gaze solemn and a little brooding.

After a couple of beats, his mouth twisted into a wry smile that reminded her of that momentary flash of loneliness she sometimes saw.

"Yeah. You know. Dinner. Where two people walk into a restaurant, sit down, order wine and a meal and then...."

He paused for a moment and just looked at her. Before

Holly could stop herself, an image of what would happen "then" popped into her head and she actually blushed. And because he wasn't blind or stupid, his eyes lit with amusement and those darn dimples made their appearance, stealing her bones and her breath.

"And then we talk."

A frisson of panic skittered up her spine. Oh, God, that was almost worse than what she'd been thinking. Almost but not quite. Because she had no intention of going "there" with him again. She was back to focusing on the fellowship and her future, neither of which had room for hunky surgeons with sexy dimples.

She nervously licked her lips and sent him a wary look. "About what?"

"About why you bailed without at least thanking me."

She blinked. "Wh-a-at?"

"And letting me thank you."

"Uh...thank you?"

He inclined his head and studied her through narrowed eyes that gleamed with a host of emotions she couldn't read. "Yep. And then we're going to talk about you."

"We are?"

"We're going to be working closely together," he pointed out quietly. "And the tension between us is bound to cause gossip I'm sure you'd rather avoid."

She sighed and swallowed the instinctive urge to say she had other plans. Which might have been the truth but if she told him she had a date with her bed, he might offer to join her there. Maybe. Or maybe he was happy with the whole "This is just a one-off thing" and just needed some friendly company.

"Fine," she said a little impatiently, but it was mostly at herself for feeling a bit insulted by his "Then we talk" comment.

Abruptly realizing that she'd dropped her cellphone, Holly sighed and turned. She really had to stop doing this.

Suspiciously quiet, Gabriel bent to retrieve it.

"What?" she demanded, when hooded eyes continued to watch as she shoved it into her purse. He shook his head, a small smile teasing the corners of his mouth as he lifted a hand and tucked a dark, errant strand of hair behind her ear.

The move, the feel of his fingertips brushing her skin, sent a shiver of longing through her. A longing so powerful that even as her nipples peaked and her breath hitched in her throat, she experienced a moment of panic. Damn it. This was precisely what she'd wanted to avoid. Being reminded of what she was missing by the "this-is-a-one-off-thing" promise she'd made.

"Any preferences?"

"For?"

An image popped into her head about preferences and she had to bite back the urge to tell him she'd liked…loved… everything he'd done. So much so that she couldn't stop thinking about him…it.

Realizing she was having hot, racy thoughts while he'd been talking about food, Holly ducked her head to hide the heat crawling up her neck into her face.

Gabriel's warm hand curled around her neck and his thumb slid beneath her chin. Very gently he lifted her face. His expression was filled with simmering heat and gentle humor. "Dinner, Holly. Just dinner. Tonight I need a friend."

After the day from hell, Gabriel had honestly planned for *just* dinner. But that had been before he'd sat across a candlelit table from her and watched her expressive face go through a host of emotions he got dizzy trying to identify. She gradually relaxed enough to smile and laugh at his stories while sharing a little of her childhood—of herself.

"Tell me about the accident," he said, when it was clear that she wasn't going to go there without some prompting from him.

Her laughter faded and he tried not to feel bad. He had

a feeling her plan to avoid everything but her career had something to do with whatever had happened to her.

She dropped her gaze to the tablecloth and fiddled with first the silverware and then her wineglass until he reached out and took her hand in his. Her fingers jerked and a fine tremor went through them.

For long moments she stared at their hands, hers delicate and pale against the tanned bulk of his. Finally she slid her hand away and reached for her wineglass again, downing the contents.

Face pale, she cleared her throat and, still not looking at him, she said, so quietly that he had to strain to hear her, "I was with a few friends at a mall and the company contracted to service the elevators had a reputation for cutting corners. Their maintenance schedule was forged and the elevators hadn't been checked in nearly a year."

She drew in a deep breath. "Well, apparently there was some malfunction that had been reported but ignored. Anyway, I…um, left my friends in the music store to go up a couple of levels to the book store and took the glass elevator because the escalators were out. On the way down I had the misfortune of picking an elevator that a noisy group of boys followed me into. The instant the doors closed they started jumping up and down, trying to frighten me."

Recalling her terror and claustrophobia, Holly paused to suck in a couple of breaths. She hated talking about it and only had nightmares when she was stressed.

"Little bastards," Gabriel muttered, and when Holly lifted her head she caught the hard light in his eyes. Strangely, that angry glitter on her behalf steadied her as sympathy could not.

"They were just kids," she excused, recalling that one of the boys had paid for that stupidity with his life. She lifted her hand in a vague gesture at her scars. "The wheel casing on the elevator car that held the cable wheel snapped and we plunged nearly three stories. There was a lot of glass and twisted steel and…and I was in the way."

After a long moment he said quietly, "It's not your fault."

Holly sighed. "I feel like I should have done something."

His eyebrow rose up his forehead. "Like?"

"Like stop them from jumping up and down."

Gabriel grimaced. "A bunch of teenage boys? Not likely."

Holly gave a small laugh of agreement and shook her head. There was nothing she could have done and she knew it.

"I guess that explains a lot."

"About?"

"Your nervousness in lifts."

Holly groaned. "That was just clumsiness on my part."

His expression was unfathomable as he slid his gaze over her face. "It could have been worse." Yes, it could. She could have died along with that other boy. "You want dessert or coffee?"

Holly let out a shuddery breath of relief. He was giving her the space she needed to get her emotions under control again without spouting off a lot of platitudes. "Coffee would be great, thank you."

Although Gabe hadn't had more than a couple glasses of wine with his meal, by the time they stood on the street outside her house he felt a little drunk. And staring into her upturned face, he discovered he couldn't keep his promise.

He couldn't let her go. Not tonight.

Yanking her against him, he closed his mouth over hers in a kiss filled with heat and a wild desperation that might have scared him if he hadn't finally had his mouth and hands on her after what felt like a lifetime of frustration.

After her initial surprise, she wrapped her arms around his neck and clung, returning his kisses with as much hunger and heat as he felt. *God.* He'd never experienced anything like it. Like she was as eager to get as close as she possibly could, maybe permanently imprint the feel, the taste and the smell of her on his senses.

Unable to resist, he drew her closer and then closer still, sliding his tongue against hers even as he molded her against him until there was nothing between them but a few too many layers of fabric.

And before he knew it they were in his house and he was pushing her roughly against his front door to ravage her mouth and slake his raging thirst.

With shaking hands they tore at each other's clothing until he could thrust a hair-roughened thigh between her silky-smooth ones and take her breast in his mouth.

Clutching at him, Holly arched her back and emitted a long low moan that grabbed his gut and gave it a vicious twist. He didn't know how they ended up on the floor in a tangle of limbs and discarded clothing. He was too busy whipping her up again and again until she was moaning and begging him to take her.

And then he did. With one hard thrust that drew a ragged moan from her throat even as she arched her back, her inner muscles clamping down on him so hard he saw stars.

He froze, eyes locked on her face.

"Did I hurt you?" he gasped, his sides heaving like he'd run the length of Manhattan Island in three minutes flat.

Looking flushed and dazed and so incredibly beautiful that Gabe had to keep a tight rein on his inclination to pound his way to completion, Holly blinked her eyes open. Damn, he thought, feeling a little dazed himself, she took his breath away.

Or maybe that was just because she was wrapped around him like a ball of twine, arching her long, curvy body and making those breathy little sounds that had the top of his head threatening to explode.

"Whydidyoustop?" she demanded in a breathless rush, sinking her nails into his back, sending shudders of pure heat streaking down his spine to his groin.

"You…" He swallowed the groan building in his chest and felt his eyes cross when she slid her inner thighs up his flanks and clenched her inner muscles around him. "Damn it… Holly…stop a minute, will you?"

Her response was to lift her head to give his lip a punishing nip. He shuddered and the last slender thread of his fraying control snapped. Grabbing her hands, he tethered them beside her head and pressed her writhing body into the floor. "Look at me," he commanded, waiting until her eyes fluttered open and locked with his.

"I want to see your eyes when you come," he growled fiercely. "I want to look at you and know I'm all you see… all you feel."

"Gabriel…"

"Just," he murmured, dropping a hard kiss on her mouth, "just as I see only you." And then with a groan that seemed to originate from somewhere near his knees Gabe withdrew only to slam back into her body as though to fuse them together for all time.

Light burst behind his eyes and Holly cried out, trying to wrench her hands free, but Gabe knew if she touched him he'd lose it big time. He was that close.

He wanted this to last. Needed it to last.

Slowly, savoring the incredible sensations of being inside her again, Gabriel withdrew and with his eyes locked on hers entered her more slowly. She gave a soft mewl and her eyes darkened to midnight. Dropping his lips to the soft spot at the base of her throat, he smiled at the feel of her pulse fluttering wildly beneath the delicate skin.

Her hands tightened into fists. "Gabriel," she pleaded softly, her breath catching when he softly kissed the outward sign of her rioting emotions. Hell, his emotions were all over the place too and when he lifted his head and stared down into her flushed face the world tilted wildly on its axis. Some inexplicably painful emotion gripped him then and before he knew what was happening he'd lost the last fragile grip on his control.

All too soon Holly was arching in his arms, her smoky gaze locked on his as he pounded into her like he couldn't get enough—would never get enough. Then her eyes went dark, blind, and with a low ragged sound she went hurling off the edge, leaving him helpless against the violent storm crashing through him.

CHAPTER TEN

HE DIDN'T KNOW how long they lay there in a tangle of limbs, damp skins clinging as their thundering hearts slowed and their ragged breathing eased.

Tiny aftershocks spasmed through her, keeping him hard until she finally drew in a shuddering breath. "Oh, God," she rasped. "Wha—?" He felt her swallow convulsively and draw in another wheezing breath. "What the hell was that?"

He grunted. Besides being the only response he could manage, he didn't have a clue either. He hadn't had nearly the number of relationships that people liked to believe but he was thirty-five years old, for God's sake. Granted, he was more experienced than he cared to admit but not even when he'd been a randy fifteen-year-old had he lost it so completely.

With a groan he got his elbows beneath him and levered the bulk of his weight off her. He was about to roll off her but he caught sight of her face and he froze. She looked dazed.

His chest squeezed and he lost his breath all over again. This time with dread. "What?" She stared at him for a couple of seconds then blinked as though coming out of a trance.

"Sorry, what?" she rasped.

He frowned, beginning to think something was seriously wrong. "Are you okay?"

Her cheeks reddened. "Define...um...okay."

"Oh, God, I hurt you, didn't I?"

"What?" Her eyes widened. "No! Why would you think that?"

"You're acting weird."

Her eyes slid away. "Oh. Well...I...um..." She paused and licked her lips, another blush working its way up her throat. Her pulse beat a rapid tattoo in her throat. "You're... heavy, is all."

"Uh-huh." He didn't buy it for a minute. Especially not now when he'd shifted most of his weight off her. "Try again."

Her gaze slide to him and then away. She licked her lips, looking adorably flustered.

"You're saying I didn't hurt you?" he pressed. She gave quick headshake and tried to wriggle away but he was still buried deep, tearing a distressed squeak from her throat when he hardened even more.

"Holly."

Her breath escaped in a loud whoosh along with an eye-roll. "You're...um...you're still hard."

A smile of pure deviltry curved his mouth. "Oh, yeah. And I'm going to take care of it. Right now."

"Now?" she asked a little breathlessly, her eyes going wide. "So soon after...well, that?"

"Oh, yeah," he repeated, his voice emerging on a low growl when her inner muscles fluttered around him. "As soon as I can move without my blood pressure shooting out the top of my head, I'm going to try and repeat that."

She giggled and smoothed her hands down over his abs to where they were locked together like two puzzle pieces. Drawing in a ragged breath, Gabe gritted his teeth and slipped out of her body. He froze when she made a tiny sound of protest then surged to his feet in one determined move.

"But I'm not doing it here," he said, reaching down to

wrap long fingers around her wrist. With a tug he hauled her to her feet, wrapping his arm around her waist when her knees threatened to buckle and dump her on her very delectable ass. She clutched at him. Okay, they clutched at each other, because if he was being perfectly honest here his knees were a little shaky too. Especially when her incredibly good parts bumped his.

"Bedroom," he croaked.

"Can't move," she managed sleepily, smoothing her hands over his flanks to his back. And in the wake of that languid caress, his skin tightened and he was suddenly impatient for her all over again.

"That's okay," he murmured against her temple. "I've got this." *I've got you.*

Unlike the last time when she'd awakened to find something heavy and deliciously warm pinning her to the bed, Holly knew exactly where she was and how she'd got there.

And like the last time Holly blamed the wine. Okay, maybe it was also because she couldn't resist dimples and wicked blue-green eyes.

She was weak.

And it was all his fault.

For two years she'd managed to concentrate on her surgical career without once forgetting her plan or losing sight of her goal. Okay, and maybe there'd been no one who had tempted her, but then Dr. Hot Stuff had flashed his package and his dimples her way.

Her breath hitched.

Darn dimples.

And darn the hard warm body currently pressed against her back—heavy arm pinning her to the bed and a large hand cupping her breast—tempting her to repeat her mistakes.

Holly didn't normally repeat mistakes but it seemed all

he had to do was ply her with food and wine and she was a goner. No more, she told herself, she was going to be strong.

Slowly, carefully, she lifted each finger and then the rest of his hand from where it cupped her breast. Just as she was about to inch out from underneath his arm he moved, pulling her back against his body. His very aroused body.

She slammed her eyes closed with a muffled little squeak, hoping he'd think she was just moving and making noises in her sleep.

"Where are you going?" His voice, a sleep-roughened rasp in her ear, had her body tingling in unmentionable places. Holly held her breath, conscious of her heart trying to punch its way through her ribcage. She wondered if he could feel it too since the panicked *boom, boom, boom* shook the bed like a five on the Richter Scale.

He moved a hair-roughened leg between hers, his huge sigh disturbing the long tangle of hair obscuring her vision. Her breath escaped in a silent hiss when she felt something hard poke into her bottom. She rolled her eyes and stifled a snicker. *Damn.* Who'd have thought the sexy surfer would be a snuggler? Or that he'd awaken with his surfboard between them.

She waited until he was breathing evenly again before easing out of his hold. Once she was clear she edged her way carefully across the huge bed and was just congratulating herself on having made a clean getaway when he said, "Do I have to tie you down?"

Slapping a hand over the shriek that emerged, Holly cast a wide-eyed look over her shoulder and caught sight of Gabriel lying sprawled across the bed in nothing but gloriously tanned skin, looking at once satiated and exasperated.

Looking better than he had any right to look after being up half the night.

Finally realizing he was studying her nudity with open interest, she gave a strangled squeak and grabbed for the sheets. Unfortunately, she had to stretch about a mile for them and because he was closer he simply snagged the soft cotton and yanked it out of reach.

Her mouth dropped open and she glared at him for a couple of beats until she realized she was caught out in the open in nothing but her Wildman from Borneo hair.

Slapping both hands over her naked breasts, Holly blew hair out of her face and narrowed her eyes as she considered her options. It was either sit there like an embarrassed virgin or get up and saunter from the room.

Buck naked, of course. Because her clothes were littered all over Gabriel's entrance floor. Again.

He must have read her mind because he simply arched his eyebrow and waited. She finally sucked in air and made a dive off the bed, but he moved like lightning and before she could clear the edge of the bed he caught her, fingers wrapped around her ankle, holding her as effectively as if she'd been shackled.

Holly gasped at discovering she was face down and hanging over the edge of the bed—*oh, boy*—her position giving Gabriel a view that made her blush.

She gave a squeak of distress because he tightened his grip and began to reel her in until she was all the way back on the bed. There was a moment of silence. She sucked in air and waited—anticipation buzzing through her blood like a swarm of excited bees.

His hand smoothed a path of fire up the back of her leg to her knee. There he paused and something brushed the soft skin. Fiery heat that she'd thought extinguished in the dark early hours of the morning arrowed right up the insides of her legs to ground zero and Holly had to bite back a whimper of need. A quick glance over her naked shoulder told her he'd kissed that tiny erogenous spot and was looking up the long length of her thigh. Right where his touch had sent an erotic message.

Squirming with embarrassment, she gasped out a horrified "What are you doing?" drawing his hooded gaze.

"You planning on bailing again?"

Darn it. She'd wondered when he'd bring that up again. "No," she squeaked, feeling her entire body blush. "I, um… I need the bathroom. Really, really badly."

Holding her gaze, he bent his head and nipped the curve of her butt. Her muscles quivered. "If you're not out in three minutes I'm coming to get you."

"What? But…but I've got to…um…go. I've got an… um, thing."

"You've got the day off," he pointed out. "Heck, you've got the next three days off and so do I." He let that news sink in before saying, "I want to you spend them with me," in a voice that washed a heady eroticism over her. But it was his expression that had Holly stilling. He was preparing for her to say no.

"You…do?"

His gaze locked with hers, his thumb brushing the curve where her bottom joined her thigh. "Yes," he said seriously. "I do."

Over the long line of her naked back Holly searched his expression then nodded. She had to swallow the huge lump lodged in her throat before she said breathlessly, "Okay, but I have to attend my father's birthday dinner tonight and I still haven't got him a gift."

"We'll go together."

Surprise had her blinking. "Shopping? Or dinner?"

"Both," he said, before abruptly stilling. After a few beats he lifted his gaze from where he'd been watching his hand rub her bottom, his expression carefully neutral. Her pulse fluttered. "Unless you don't want me to meet your family." His hand slid away and he sat up, looking all hot and naked and pissy. "Unless you already have a date."

"No!" She turned, wondering what that was all about. But she had other things to consider. Like how she would introduce him to her family. Her mother would be over the moon that Holly had a date and would start reading all sorts of things into it, but Paige…? Unless…

Her belly quivered and she racked her brains, trying to remember if her mother had said anything about Paige being off displaying her expensive body for the camera somewhere.

The last she'd heard, her sister was in Fiji with her current lover. Holly hoped she stayed there.

In fact, taking Gabe to dinner would solve a lot of problems, the most urgent one being her mother. Delia kept throwing men at Holly like confetti, hoping she would find one acceptable, marry and give her more grandkids to dote on.

"No," she said again, this time more calmly as she mulled the idea over in her head. Not only would it keep her mother off her back but she wouldn't feel like a permanent fifth wheel. Or that awkward nerdy kid dragged to every social engagement against her will.

A smile grew. "I think that's a great idea." She paused and frowned as she thought about what it would be like for him. "Are you sure you want to be bored…? I mean, it's just family."

Gabriel's expression darkened. "You don't think I'll fit in?"

She rolled her eyes and huffed out a laugh. "God, no." Then, seeing his face, she hurried to explain. "That's a good thing, believe me."

"It is?"

"Heck, most of the time I don't fit in. Especially if my sister's there and if mother's invited all their friends." She made a face. "Believe me, boredom is nothing to what you're likely to experience with a bunch of dry attorneys and judges discussing the law." She shuddered. "If it wasn't my father's birthday, I'd invent something serious and cry off."

After a long moment during which his blue-green eyes

searched hers Gabriel nodded, a small smile lifting one corner of his mouth. "Okay, then," he murmured softly, reaching out to snag her hand. He yanked her down and rolled
her beneath him, his eyes hot and heavy. "What should we
do in the meantime?"

If Gabe had forgotten exactly where Holly had come from,
her childhood home reminded him. Set in the town of Stony
Brook, Long Island, it screamed old money. Surrounded by
expansive lawns and trees heavy with autumn foliage it was
everything he would have had if not for Caspar Alexander.

Pulling the rental to stop in the sweeping drive, he shook
off his odd mood and ignored the fact that he might be nervous. He wasn't. He had nothing to be nervous about. He
might enjoy spending time with Holly Buchanan—in and
out of bed—but he knew from experience that he wasn't in
any danger of falling for her. At least, not the forever kind.
Beside him she drew in a deep breath before flashing him
a brave smile. "You ready?"

She's nervous, he thought, exiting the luxury vehicle and
rounding the hood to open the passenger door. She nibbled
on her bottom lip, looking uncertain, which prompted him
to ask, "The question is, are you?"

"Me?" She shrugged, looking stunning in a dark blue
silky sheath the color of her eyes. "They're my family."
She drew in a deep breath, expelling it in a long whoosh
when he grabbed her hand and drew her from the vehicle.
"They can just be a little overwhelming…and protective,"
she warned. "My mother especially. She'll probably hug
you and maybe flirt a little."

"That's okay, Holly." He smiled, giving her hand a reassuring squeeze. "I'm good with that, especially if she's as
beautiful as you."

"Oh, I'm nothing like my mother," she said with a laugh,
and turned to gather up her purse and her father's expertly
wrapped gift. "She's beautiful and loves people—really

loves having them around. She doesn't look a day over forty and people often mistake her for Paige's older sister. My mother loves it but Paige?" She gave a short laugh. "Well, Paige's another matter altogether."

Before they'd taken a dozen steps a tall, slender blonde burst out of the house and swept down the stairs to gather Holly into a fierce hug. "Oh, my darling, I'm so glad you're here."

With such evident emotion shining in her beautiful face, there was no doubt that Delia Buchanan loved her daughter. Gabe felt his chest tighten and lifted a hand to rub the ache that settled next to his heart. He hadn't realized until this moment just how much he missed his mother and wondered if Holly knew how lucky she was.

Delia moved back to plant a kiss on each of Holly's cheeks. "Your father's going to be thrilled. It's been an age since you were home," she said chidingly.

"Hi, Mom," Holly said, kissing her mother's cheek. "Missed you too."

"Oh, let me look at you," she murmured, drawing back to study Holly's face. Her eyes, so much like Holly's, widened. "Oh, darling, you're...glowing. And since you left word with Rosa that you're bringing someone I guess I owe him for that."

She turned toward Gabriel and he got his first good look at the ex-beauty queen. She was indeed stunning and so much like Holly that he could understand people mistaking the two of *them* for sisters, as they had very similar bone structure and the same eyes.

She squirmed. "We just spent the day on Staten Island and the ferry...and, well, stuff. Gabriel's a...a surgeon."

He arched his brow at her a little challengingly but she sent him a desperate look that begged him to back her up.

"Don't be silly, darling. If anyone can get you out of that hospital and into the glorious fall air then I'm over the moon with gratitude." Still clutching her daughter's hand, she smiled at Gabe. It lit her entire face from within, exactly the way Holly's did. "And he's so handsome too, darling. Where did you find him?"

Holly blushed and elbowed her mother. "Mom, jeez. He's standing right there."

"I know," Delia said, sounding thrilled. "Isn't it wonderful? Oh, don't mind me." She laughed, taking Gabe's face in her hands and reaching up to kiss his cheek. "It's simply been an age since Holly was home, let alone brought a date."

"It's a pleasure to meet you, Mrs. Buchanan. I hope I'm not intruding on your family occasion."

"It's Delia, and don't be silly." She tucked her hand into the crook of his elbow and led him up the stairs to the front door, leaving Holly to follow. "It's just family and a few close friends. Bryant and Richard are here so you won't feel like you're the only young man among all the stodgy old men."

"It's been a long time since a beautiful woman called me a young man," Gabe said, smiling over his shoulder at Holly, who rolled her eyes and bumped the front door closed with her hip. "I can see where Holly gets her sweet nature."

There was a short silence and then both Holly and her mother burst out laughing. Delia grinned at him, gave him a fierce hug. "Oh, you're sweet. I think we'll keep you." She turned to Holly. "Darling, why don't you two go on into the salon? I'm just seeing to some last-minute food emergencies and your father's sitting around like a king waiting for his adoring subjects. And if he's smoking those awful cigars, remind him about what the doctor said."

Once Delia disappeared, Gabe drew in a deep breath and turned to Holly with a look of confusion. "I did warn you."

"No, I'm confused by the laughter."

"Oh, that." She shrugged. "No one's ever called me sweet before. Believe me," she added, when he arched his brow, "I was a really difficult kid. I was skinny as a pole, wore glasses and braces and I was forever walking into things and tripping over my feet. I used to hide when it was time to attend social functions."

Gabe's mouth curled up at one side and he let his gaze slide over her, from the intricate twist she'd managed to coax her long dark hair into, over her face and breasts to the slender, curvy body and dark blue strappy heels that made her legs look incredibly long.

"Well…maybe you're still a little accident-prone but no one could call you a pole and…" he leaned forward to add into her ear "…I know exactly how sweet you are. *All* over. Especially that spot…"

"Now, this," a coolly amused voice came from somewhere over Holly's shoulder, "is the true meaning of sweet." Feeling Holly stiffen, he flicked a curious look over her shoulder. In the middle of the stairs leading to the upper floors—and illuminated as though she stood in a spotlight for maximum effect—was a woman Gabe couldn't help but recognize. He'd have to be living in Outer Mongolia not to recognize supermodel Paige. And suddenly those weird flashes of familiarity made sense. Not to mention he'd also done a host of cosmetic procedures on the woman a couple of years ago.

Conscious of the odd tension pulsing off Holly, he straightened, watching as Paige Buchanan swept down the stairs in something long and floaty, trailing her hand on the banister as she descended. "Ms. Buchanan."

"Oh, Gabriel," she sighed with a pout as she floated closer, reaching up to pat his cheek. "There's really no need for all the formality. Besides, you've seen me naked and had your hands on my breasts…and…well, everywhere else." She blushed prettily and fluttered her lashes, before looking up at him in a move he remembered as being a tad overdone. It was as if she was constantly playing to an invisible camera. Her hand touched his arm. "And now here you are, with…Holly? That is surprising." She finally turned to her sister and did the air-kiss thing as Holly stood looking suddenly remote and cool. "Oh, sis," Paige crooned. "I'd love to hear how you two met. I'll bet it's an…interesting story."

"Not so interesting," Holly said smoothly, sending Gabe a hooded glance that he found difficult to read when before she'd been an open book. He narrowed his eyes on her, wondering at the undercurrents suddenly swirling around him like a thick fog, as well as the white-knuckled grip she had on the gift she clutched. "Gabriel's taken the opening in Plastic and Reconstruction."

Paige's smile widened. "Well, now, that's an amazing co-incidence as I'm thinking about having a few things done."

Out the corner of his eye Gabe caught Holly's eye-roll. "I don't do cosmetics anymore," he told the model. "Dr. Syu at West Manhattan is an excellent cosmetic surgeon. Besides, you're beautiful enough without resorting to surgery. I told you that before."

"I don't want Lin Syu," she said, gazing up at him imploringly. "I want the best." She sent Holly a quick look under her lashes. "I want you." And for some odd reason Gabe got the impression she was talking about something else entirely. "Besides, it's just a few minor tweaks. Anyway…" She suddenly tugged playfully at his arm and drew him toward the double wooden doors to Gabe's left. "Do you have a drink? I can't believe Holly hasn't offered you a drink yet."

"We only just arrived," he said coolly, casting a look over his shoulder in time to see Holly's expression go carefully blank as if all the vitality had been sucked out of her. "In fact, we were on our way to see your father."

"Oh, don't worry about that. Holly will handle it and you can meet Daddy later. Besides, I'm parched and I'll just bet you are too."

Gabe was startled by the barely concealed hostility. "No. I—"

"It's fine," Holly said without expression. "You go ahead.

I'll just…" She gestured to her right before turning and hurrying down a short passage.

Gabe resisted Paige's attempts to pull him through the doors. Carefully removing her hand from his arm, he turned and narrowed his eyes at her.

"What was that all about, Ms. Buchanan?"

She looked startled. "I…I don't know what you mean."

"That little show you put on for Holly."

A secret little smile tugged at her famous mouth and she snuggled close, pressing her equally famous breasts—that he'd provided—against his arm. "Oh, relax. It's just a little game we play. We bring dates home and the other tries to lure them away. She does it all the time."

Gabe sincerely doubted that. His skepticism must have shown because Paige laughed, looking incredibly beautiful but to his discerning eye there was something off with her. A hardness in her eyes, a brittleness to her laugh.

"Oh, come on," she wheedled. "Let's have a drink. I'm in a party mood. Besides, Holly will be presenting Daddy with her incredibly thoughtful gift and hoping for a little paternal attention." She rolled her eyes. "You don't want to see that, believe me. It's nauseating in its desperation. And," she drawled lightly, "I've resolved never to gag before dinner."

CHAPTER ELEVEN

HOLLY FOUND HER father in his den with a couple of his closest friends, puffing on cigars and talking shop. Her breath caught in her throat, just as it used to when she was little and couldn't believe that such a handsome man was her father. Just as it did whenever she approached his den, wondering if he would even remember her name.

He was laughing as he turned and caught sight of her hovering in the doorway. "Holly," he said, discarding the cigar and dropping a brief kiss on her cheek when she stepped into the room.

"Happy birthday, Dad," she murmured, handing him his gift.

"I bet old Bergen wishes he was half as beautiful as you," her father's oldest friend said when he hugged Holly. "It might sweeten his disposition." He turned to the room. "Isn't she just like her mother?"

"The spitting image."

Holly rolled her eyes. It was a ritual everyone in the room had played since she'd been a shy, withdrawn teenager.

"When can I make an appointment?" her father's senior partner said, rising to greet her. "My foot is bothering me again. I need a second opinion."

Laughing, she hugged the old man. "If you're thinking about a facial reconstruction, Uncle Franklin, I'm your girl. But if you want to improve your fasciitis, you'll have to stop drinking red wine and smoking those cigars. Oh, and you might want to cut back on the red meat."

"You're as bad as Dr. Bergen," Franklin said in disgust, but his eyes twinkled, making Holly laugh.

"The girl's right, Frank," another partner added cheerfully. "Maybe a facial reconstruction will help. God knows, Sophie would probably approve. She might even agree to that second honeymoon you've been talking about."

With laughter filling the room, Holly left them to shop-talk. She headed for the salon and found Gabriel with her brother, Bryant, while Holly's sister-in-law chatted to the other guests. He looked perfectly content with Paige cleaved to his side like a surgical skin graft. But, then, why wouldn't he? Paige drew men like flies to a cadaver. She was beautiful, fun and exciting. According to a top men's magazine she'd also been voted as one of the ten sexiest women in the world. What man would want to look at—be with—*her* when Paige was around?

He looked up and smiled when he saw her but Paige pulled on his arm to get his attention. With her eyes on Holly, she leaned into him and reached up to brush some non-existent lint from his lapel before smoothing her palm down his abdomen to the waistband of his pants.

It was a game her sister had played since they'd been teenagers and suddenly her head was pounding like she'd spent the day drinking mojitos. She knew exactly how hard and touchable Gabriel's abs were and hated...really, *really* hated seeing her sister slide her hands over him as if she had the right, all the while silently challenging Holly with her eyes.

"Go over there and get your man," Delia murmured, slipping her arm around Holly's waist.

"He's not my man, Mom," she said wearily, and lifted shaking fingers to rub at the pain blossoming behind her eyes. "We're just colleagues."

"Oh, honey, I saw the way he looked at you and—"

"Yeah," she interrupted, turning away from the concern in her mother's gaze. "He's wondering how to ditch me so he can have Paige."

"Oh, my sweet girl. No, don't you look at me like that, Holly Noël Buchanan," Delia snapped. "You are sweet. I know we joke about it but you are, even when you're being an idiot."

Holly sent her mother a half-smile. "You have to say that, Mom, you're my mother. But I can't compete with Paige. I never could, and you know it. No, Mom, don't," she said wearily, when her mother looked like she was about to object, vehemently. "Let's be honest here, not many women can compete with someone on the top ten sexiest women list."

"You're not just any woman, Holly," Delia snapped. "And being sexy is more than flashing your body and pouting for a camera."

"It made her famous."

"It also made her spoiled," Delia said firmly. "For which I blame myself."

"It's not your fault, Mom. Paige always craved attention. She got it."

"And you shunned it."

"I liked books more. Anyway," she sighed, waving her hand dismissively, "I was just wondering what happened to Darian. I thought she was over the moon in love and planning to become Mrs. Darian Something…and now here she is." *All over my date.*

"It was Andreas," Delia corrected quietly, and Holly could see her mother's concern for Paige in her worried expression. "Darian was the one before." She sighed. "And like Darian, Andreas apparently forgot to mention that he was already married."

Holly rolled her eyes and nearly yelped when her brain threatened to explode inside her skull. She didn't say what was obvious to them both: Paige liked taking other women's men. It made her feel powerful and...desirable. And now it looked like she wanted Holly's. Again.

If only to prove she could.

Not that Gabriel was hers, she amended quickly. Two incredible nights didn't make him hers any more than it made her his. He was free to do anything he wanted and she...well, she'd had her exercise and now it was back to her plan. A plan that didn't include getting worked up over a man who could make women scream one minute and cozy up to another the next.

Holly pretended, for her mother's sake, to have a wonderful time but she couldn't wait for the evening to end. Her sister had somehow switched the name settings so she could sit next to Gabriel, whom she proceeded to manipulate with soft touches, coy looks and, Holly was certain, feeling him up beneath the tablecloth. Heck, she'd seen it all before. A hundred times.

Holly sat between Franklin and Richard Westchester, the son of a family friend that Delia had invited before Holly had called to say she was bringing a date. And if she smiled a little too brightly at Rick and leaned toward him a little too closely, Holly told herself it was simply because she was being a gracious dinner companion. It certainly wasn't because Gabriel was being attentive to Paige or watching *her* with a brooding expression.

The instant dinner was over she shoved back from the table and quietly excused herself. Her head throbbed like an open head wound and she headed upstairs to her parents' bathroom.

After downing pain meds and splashing her face with cool water, she made for the French doors that led to the balcony. Maybe a little fresh air and alone time would help soothe her aching head before she put on her game face and returned downstairs.

She let herself out and shivered in the cool night air but it was dark and quiet. Wrapping her arms around herself to ward off the chill, she leaned her hot forehead against the old stone pillar, staring out across the lawn toward the water.

She'd been out there a minute only when she became aware of murmured voices. One deep and achingly familiar, the other...well, it wasn't a surprise to hear her sister's smoothly amused tones.

She didn't mean to eavesdrop and wasn't in the least bit interested in Paige's plans to have some imaginary defect fixed, but when she heard her name she couldn't help peering over the balustrade and holding her breath so she could listen.

Paige was draped artfully in a pose she often used to display her amazing body to maximum effect. She took a sip of champagne from the flute she'd brought from the dinner table and Holly had to wonder how many times it had been refilled. She wondered too if her mother had noticed that as dinner had progressed, Paige had become more and more flushed and animated.

Watching now, she saw Paige tip back her head, luxurious waves of silvery blonde hair cascading over her naked shoulders. For a moment she thought Paige looked right at her and although she was in deep shadow, Holly drew further into the darkness.

"I came with Holly," she heard Gabriel say. "What do you want, Paige?"

"I just needed some fresh air and as I'm not feeling well..." her breath hitched dramatically "...I thought having a doctor around would help."

"You don't need a doctor to tell you that laying off the champagne would help."

Paige gave a dramatic sigh and set her glass aside before pushing away from the balustrade. "You're right," she purred, sliding her hands over Gabriel's chest and linking her arms behind his neck to smile up into his face. "You've got me. I know you came with Holly, but it's clear she's otherwise occupied and…well, I just didn't want you to feel left out, that's all."

Holly wondered if she was the only one who'd noticed that Paige had been the one feeling left out, which was why she'd attached herself to the best-looking man in the group.

"I saw you change the seating arrangements," he observed, putting his hands on her waist, whether to push her away or an excuse to touch her Holly couldn't tell. "I wondered about your motive."

"Oh, Richard's such a bore. I can't understand why Mother insists on inviting him but, then, I suppose it's because Holly always had a thing for him. Besides…" she pouted charmingly "…I just wanted you to myself without her watching every move I make. She's incredibly…possessive for someone who claims you're just colleagues."

"She said that?"

She shrugged. "Anyway, I thought I might convince you to change your mind about doing me that teensy favor."

"I've already told you I don't do cosmetic surgery anymore, Paige. Besides, I'm booked solid for the next six months. Probably longer."

Annoyance flashed across her features and she spun away to say sulkily, "Fine, then maybe you can use your incredible sex appeal to persuade Holly to have a little work done."

"Work?"

Light spilling from the salon illuminated Paige's face, giving Holly a clear view of the flirtatious look she sent over her shoulder. She gave a little laugh and turned back to slide her palm over his heart. "Don't pretend they're invisible, Gabriel." She shuddered delicately. "Those scars are awful and people don't realize how hurtful pitying stares are. In fact, I used to feel so bad when boys called her Scarface that I wondered if you could persuade her to have them…fixed?"

Like hell she'd felt bad, Holly thought darkly. She'd

laughed, telling Holly she should have an infamous comic book badass named after her.

"Hmm..." Gabriel rocked back on his heels as though he was considering her words.

Holly sucked in a sharp breath, the betrayal like a blow to her heart. She couldn't believe that after kissing every one of those scars, moving his lips against her skin and murmuring that she was beautiful, he— She bit her lip. Clearly, after seeing Paige's flawless beauty, he was reconsidering.

She pressed the heel of her hand to the spot between her brows as pain lanced through her head. Oh, God, she needed to get out of here. Away from...them. Away somewhere where she could fall apart in private.

She was about to turn away when she heard him say, "So what else would you suggest she have...done?"

Feeling the backs of her eyes burn, she waited with a huge hot lump of devastation in her chest for her sister's reply. When it came, it sliced at the self-confidence she'd spent so many years trying to build. And even though she understood that Paige's opinions reflected her own insecurities and jealousy, it made Holly feel like the ugly adopted sister Paige had always called her.

"Well," Paige said demurely, "I was thinking a breast lift and maybe since her hips and thighs are getting chunky, a little lipo? And she could certainly do with a nose job. What do you think?"

And when Gabriel laughed and said, "Chunky? You really think so?" she couldn't listen anymore because Paige reached up and twined her fingers in his hair.

His hands came up to her shoulders and the sight of them plastered together like a seal-a-meal ripped at the tender new feelings that had been blossoming inside her chest. But she couldn't...*couldn't* bear to listen to every one of her flaws discussed like a grocery list. She'd survived it once before when Paige had slept with and then dumped Holly's last boyfriend and she would survive it again.

Right now she couldn't bear to stick around and watch it happening again.

The last twenty-four hours had been fun but it was over and time to return to the real world. Time to return to planning for her future and time she forgot about a hunky surfer from California. No matter how hot he was or how good he was with his hands. And his lips.

Oh, God.

Turning, she walked blindly into the safety of her parents' bedroom, her mind spinning as she wondered how she was going to make a clean getaway. There wasn't time to fall apart however, as Delia entered as she was closing the French doors.

"There you are, darling," she said, catching sight of her. "We're getting ready to serve coffee so your father can blow out his candles." Holly turned and her mother stopped abruptly, her eyes widening when she caught sight of her expression. "I'm going to slap that girl," Delia said fiercely. "She's not too old for it."

"Mom…it's fine. Really," she insisted, when her mother opened her mouth to object. "Besides, I'm not feeling well and I wondered if you'd please tell Dad I'm sorry and make my apologies to everyone else?"

She searched Holly's face and then sighed, her eyes filled with so much compassionate concern that Holly was tempted to walk into Delia's arms and bawl. But that would only upset her mother more.

"All right, darling," Delia agreed softly, "but I think you're making a terrible mistake. I like him and…well, I guess I shouldn't interfere." She rolled her eyes before turning with a muttered "I promised myself I wouldn't interfere." Then over her shoulder she asked gently, "Do you want me to ask Gabriel to take you home?"

"No!" she yelped, and when her mother's eyebrow rose, she said more quietly. "Please, Mom…don't. I just…I…" She

heaved out a heavy breath and tried to wrestle her spinning emotions into submission. "I'll call a cab. You can tell Gabriel the hospital called."

For a long moment her mother silently studied her until Holly thought she might break down beneath that blue gaze. Finally she stepped closer and gave Holly a warm hug. "All right," she murmured softly, "but you're not calling a cab. I'll ask Richard to drive you back to the city."

Holly's eyes abruptly filled but she drew in a deep breath and willed away the tears. "Thanks, Mom."

Gabe was furious—with Holly for leaving without a word and with Paige for her machinations. But mostly he was furious with himself for thinking Holly was different. He also felt very bad for Delia Buchanan, who'd seemed genuinely upset when she gave him Holly's message.

"I'm so sorry, Gabriel," she said, taking his hands in hers.

"You have nothing to be sorry about, Mrs. Buchanan," he said. "This is not on you."

"No," she agreed quietly. "It's on both my daughters and I'm very sorry you got caught in the middle. Paige...well, Paige was always incredibly jealous of Holly even as a child, and after a while it was just easier for Holly to withdraw and let Paige have her way."

"That's insane."

"Yes, well," she said with a sad smile. "Paige is beautiful but there's just something a little fragile in her make-up. Holly was always the strong one, even when she was so adorably skinny and clumsy. She was smart and funny but couldn't get the hang of all those coltish arms and legs. I tried to help with ballet lessons, deportment and acting classes but I fear I just made things worse."

"You did what any mother would do," Gabe said, recalling the sacrifices his own mother had made for him. "But she's made her feelings perfectly clear."

"Yes, she has," Delia said sympathetically, laying her hand on his tense arm. "And you've misinterpreted her actions."

"How can I misinterpret the way she acted with Westchester during dinner or that she left with him the minute it was over?" he demanded, feeling once again like that poor med student invited to the mansion and humiliated by Lauren's family's condescending attitude.

"You appeared engrossed with Paige," she reminded him gently. "And for Holly at least, it seemed like history repeating itself all over again. So she did what she's always done when it comes to Paige. She withdrew. But I know she cares for you, Gabriel. She wouldn't have invited you or gone off like that if she didn't."

Sighing, Gabe thrust a hand through his hair. He didn't know what to think.

"Don't give up on her," Delia begged softly. "Get her to talk to you, please. And for God's sake don't get sucked into Paige's dramas. She has a bad habit of wanting what Holly has and destroying everything good in her own life."

But Holly didn't have him, Gabe thought furiously as he drove back to the city. She'd made it perfectly clear that she preferred someone from her own social circle. Someone from old money and an ancestry that could probably be traced back to Ellis Island. Maybe the Buchanan sisters were letting their history repeat itself but there was no way he was going to make the same mistake.

Not again, he vowed fiercely as Holly's phone again went to voicemail. He ground his back teeth together until his jaw popped.

Great. Now he was grinding his teeth into powder.

Disconnecting with a short jab, he ignored the angry honking around him and whipped across three lanes to take the Brooklyn exit. He was done with women, and he was especially done with Holly Buchanan.

So why, when he got home and smelled her on his pillow, did he get a hollow feeling in his chest that felt very much like grief? It wasn't, he told himself, lurching off the bed to strip the sheets and pillowcases.

It was humiliation and disgust with himself that he never seemed to learn his lesson. He was still hankering after women from the world his grandfather had denied him. Well, he was done with it, with her, he told himself as he threw himself across the freshly made bed that he'd shared with her. Twice. Which didn't explain why it suddenly felt so damn cold and…empty. Or why he couldn't stop thinking about her with another man.

He really hated thinking about her with—

Damn it!

He grabbed his phone and after a couple of indecisive beats hit redial. She'd done him a favor, he told himself, growling with frustration when the call again went to voicemail. Done him a favor by reminding him that he couldn't rely on anyone but himself and the professional reputation he'd earned through his own hard work and skill.

It had landed him the job of his dreams and he wasn't going to screw it up, especially not over some woman with big blue eyes that exposed her every thought and emotion. A woman who was soft and sweet even when she thought she wasn't. A woman who had a habit of falling at his feet and quoting random facts when she was flustered. A woman who— He stopped breathing and stared into the darkened room as the truth finally dawned.

Oh, man, he thought when he realized his mouth was curved into a sappy grin, he was in trouble. The kind of trouble that started with *L*.

His breath expelled in a hard, dry laugh.

He might as well go out and shoot himself.

CHAPTER TWELVE

INSTEAD OF GOING back to Brooklyn, Holly had Richard drop her off at her grandmother's summer house in Bay Shore. He offered to keep her company but she declined. She needed to be alone to work on her shaky defenses before facing Gabriel on Monday.

But when Monday rolled around, all Holly had to show for her days off were dark circles under her eyes and a bone-deep certainty that there was no way she could accept a fellowship in the same hospital—*oh, God, the same department*—as Gabriel. And as much as she hated the idea, she needed to review her options. And fast.

She spent the next week researching P&R programs in other cities while avoiding everyone, including her mother. She just happened to quite successfully avoid Gabriel too. Not that he'd come looking for her, she admitted with a pang. But, then, she hadn't returned his calls, even when he'd left a dozen *"Call me"* messages. And if she'd listened to his voice over and over again as she'd lain in bed at night, it hadn't been because she'd been yearning for the sound of his voice or the smell and feel of his body against hers.

He finally stopped calling and when she caught herself scouring the papers for pictures of Paige, or holding her breath every time her phone rang, she realized she'd been secretly hoping he'd... Well, she didn't know exactly, only that she'd hoped he wouldn't quit.

But he had. So…that was that, then.

The week was frantically busy. She stood in for another cosmetic surgeon whose wife went into early labor and ended up with more than enough to keep her busy and too tired at the end of each day to stay awake and brood.

The week leading up to the Chrysalis Foundation's annual charity ball she wasn't so lucky. On Tuesday she was called to Theatre for two late-night procedures when Gabriel's scheduled assistant called in with stomach flu. And because everyone was way behind schedule, Dr. Hunt assigned Holly to pick up the slack.

Fortunately there wasn't time for him to do more than study her with a penetrating blue-green gaze that made her heart flop around in her chest like a landed catfish and make quiet suggestions or give orders that everyone—including Holly—snapped to obey.

During the last stages of the second procedure, on a guy who had gynecomastia and wanted his man boobs removed, he was called away, leaving Holly to finish up the routine procedure.

She didn't see him again until late Friday afternoon as she left the surgical ward.

Scrolling through the dozen messages Delia had left about her dress and shoes for the ball, as well as her tickets, Holly rolled her eyes at her mother's OCD and…walked into a wall of living muscle and bone.

Startled, she lurched backwards—okay, shrieked and jumped about a foot in the air—and bumped into a nearby medicine trolley that hadn't been wheel-locked. A hand shot out to grab her but she yanked her arm away, the abrupt move sending the trolley skidding out from under her. She fell hard against the sluice trolley and went down in a tangle of limbs, another shriek and—yay—a half-dozen bedpans that crashed around her like the sounding of the Apocalypse.

For a couple of beats she lay there stunned until she became aware of two things. One: her notes were fluttering to the floor like confetti and, two—*oh, God*—Gabriel was dropping to his haunches beside her. Through the roaring in her ears she thought she heard him ask repeatedly if she was all right.

Realizing he was feeling her up, she jolted like she'd been shot. "What…what the heck are you doing?" she gasped on a rising inflection, shoving at his hands.

But he brushed her aside and growled, "Damn it, Holly. Stay still until I'm satisfied you're—"

The door burst open and three nurses spilled out, coming to an abrupt halt when they saw Holly flat on her bottom, bedpans and folio paper scattered all over the floor—and Gabriel Alexander's hands high up on her inner thigh.

Their eyes bugged.

"Dr. Buchanan?"

"Dr. Alexander?"

"Omigosh, are you all right?"

Sucking in a breath, she did a lightning-quick assessment and decided that other than her bruised bottom and her battered pride she was fine. "I'm…fine," she said, shoving Gabriel away and scrambling to her feet to hide her hot face.

Gabriel shot out a hand to steady her when she swayed and though she stiffened she didn't pull away. She did a mental eye-roll. Not after what had just happened—all because she hadn't wanted him to touch her.

"What happened?" the head nurse demanded, popping her head out the door and frowning at the debris scattered across the floor.

"The brake was off the meds trolley," Gabriel said, his voice more steely than she'd ever heard it.

"No," Holly hastened to say. "It was my fault. I wasn't looking where I was going and Dr. Alexander had to save me from—"

"It's not all right," he interrupted tersely. "Dr. Buchanan could have been seriously injured because someone didn't follow safety procedures." He frowned at the head nurse as the others scurried to pick up the scattered bedpans.

"Dr. Alexander—"

"Leave the papers," he ordered tersely, ignoring Holly's attempts to smooth over the situation. "I'll help Dr. Buchanan collect them."

Once the bedpans had been returned to their place and the trolleys locked, he waited until the frosted door closed on the cowed nurses before releasing his grip on Holly.

Without speaking, she dropped to her haunches and silently began gathering up her notes. She was shaking inside and had to bite her lip against the pain radiating from her elbow. She tried to hurry, wanting to escape without making even more of a fool of herself.

Unfortunately it was *waa-aay* too late for that.

She was on her knees when they both reached for the last page. Holly froze. With her heart in her throat, she was compelled to lift her gaze to his—and felt herself fall all over again. This time into a pair of blue-green eyes. *Déjà vu.* Blue-green eyes that swept over her face as though they'd been starved of the sight of her.

"Holly," he said coolly, his face expressionless. But there was a wealth of emotion in his eyes—anger, frustration, accusation, even concern, and something so dark and hot it sent hurt slicing through her.

Swallowing the sob that rose into her throat, she shook her head, snatching at the pages in his hand before surging to her feet in one smooth move. She abruptly swung on her heel and surprised herself by not falling flat on her face. Before she could stomp off with her head held high, he grabbed her arm.

Instantly pain ricocheted from her elbow to her shoulder and she flinched, unable to prevent a gasp from escaping.

He immediately released her. "What? What's wrong?"

Tears—that had little to do with the pain in her elbow— blinded her and she shook her head again and turned her face away. "Nothing. It's nothing. I just bruised my elbow, that's all."

"Let me see."

"No." She sucked in a steadying breath and said it again, this time quietly. "No. It's nothing, really. I'll be fine." She wasn't talking about her elbow. At least, not just.

"Fine, but we need to talk."

She gulped and thought, *Go away, Gabriel, can't you see I'm having a mini-freak-out here?* "There's nothing to say, Dr. Alexander."

His eyebrows flattened across the bridge of his nose and his lips firmed. "What's that supposed to mean?"

"It means you've already said everything I need to hear."

"What?" He looked so confused Holly almost relented but then she recalled the sight of her sister clinging to Gabe and her resolve hardened.

Folding her arms beneath her breasts, she thrust out her chin in silent challenge. "To Paige."

He rubbed the lines of exhaustion between his eyes and Holly was tempted to reach out and smooth them away. "Paige?" he demanded testily. "What the hell does Paige have to do with anything?"

Holly's mouth dropped open. "You're kidding, right?" Her hands curled into tight fists to keep her from taking a swing at his thick head. Maybe jolt his memory? Knock him out?

"I honestly have no idea—" He abruptly shook his head as though to clear it. "What about Westchester?"

She tried to look innocent. "What about Richard?"

"Yeah, right. It's fine to find fault with me when you ran off with him, leaving me to face your mother. Do you have any idea how humiliating that was? For both of us?"

"No more humiliating," she snapped, "than you discussing me…my scars." *Not to mention devastating.* She sucked in a steadying breath when she realized she was starting to hyperventilate. "Not to mention my sagging breasts and my huge ass and thighs!" She lowered her voice to a fierce whisper when a couple of nurses passed, eyeing them with avid curiosity. "With my sister?" She jabbed a finger at him and hissed, "My sister!"

He had the grace to wince. "You heard that?"

Suddenly Holly was exhausted. She'd been functioning on pure adrenaline since that night and she wanted to curl up in a ball and sleep for a month.

"Of course I heard it," she said wearily. "Paige made certain I heard it. Like she made certain I saw how she touched you and plastered herself..." She sucked in a steadying breath. "And how you did nothing...*nothing*...to stop her."

Her phone rang and she checked the caller ID, viciously punching the disconnect button when she saw who it was.

"Now, just a minute," he said incredulously. "*That's* what this is all about?"

Holly glared at him.

"*Damn it!* I can't believe—!" He broke off with a muttered oath and shoved his hands through his hair, looking agitated and...and hot, damn him. "Did you...did you hear everything I said to Paige out on the terrace?"

"I...I heard enough," she snapped. "Enough to know you agreed with her. But that's okay since it's nothing I haven't heard before," she said coolly. "A million times. But I can't believe you agreed with her. Not after—"

Fortunately Gabriel's furious "I did nothing of the sort" interrupted what she was going to say. Then her phone rang again and she was just about to throw the thing against the wall when she realized it wasn't Paige this time but her mother. "You know what, never mind. I have to go."

"We need to talk."

"I hardly think—"

His hand closed over her shoulder and whipped her around. "We're going to have that talk," he said firmly, his eyes glittering with determination and something else that Holly couldn't identify. It made her stomach drop then bounce back up like she'd fallen from the top of the Empire State building.

"I have to go. My mother's sent a car to take me to the hotel. I'm helping with the last minute details of the charity auction for the ball tonight," she explained when he looked like he wanted to throttle her.

"Fine," he said shortly. "I'll see you there. Save all your dances for me."

"You have an invitation?" she asked, mouth dropping open. She shook her head. Of course he had an invitation. "I mean, I might not have time—"

"I'll see you there," he ground out an instant before he yanked her against him and slammed his mouth down on hers in a hard, punishing kiss. It stunned her with its heated ferocity and even after he'd shoved back and disappeared into the surgical ward she stood open-mouthed, wide-eyed and more than a little dazed.

He'd tasted of anger and frustration, she thought dizzily. And a wild, wild lust that had just a hint of what she thought was desperation. But that was ridiculous. Wasn't it?

It took a passing med student asking, "You gonna answer that, Dr. Buchanan?" to realize she was staring at her buzzing phone as though she'd never seen it before.

A look at caller ID galvanized her into action. Once Delia Buchanan was on a roll, it took a force of nature to stop her.

Gabriel paid the cab driver and turned to look up at the blazingly bright façade of Manhattan's finest hotel. It figured that the charity foundation, which he now knew was run by Delia Buchanan, would host it here. Its five-star rating, as well as the richly appointed furnishings, would draw New York's social and moneyed elite.

It was clear by the number of glittery ballgowns and designer tuxes that the elite had converged on Manhattan for the prestigious occasion. Gabriel entered the hotel and was immediately struck by the intricate laylight high overhead, brilliantly illuminated and casting a rich warm glow over the huge lobby.

He'd stayed at the hotel only once before, when he'd flown out to see the chief of surgery, P&R head and the hospital CEO about heading up their special cases team. He hadn't seen it filled with so many bejeweled women in long glittery dresses or starched stiffs then, and despite the reek of money and breeding all but choking the atmosphere he had to admit he was impressed as hell.

Delia Buchanan must be very pleased with the turnout, he thought. He just hoped she was even more pleased when the contributions came pouring in.

He nodded to a couple of hospital board members gathered near the entrance and paused on the threshold. The enormous neoclassical ballroom had recently been renovated to its original opulence, a perfect setting for dining in splendor and emptying out fat wallets.

Gabe wondered what little Lacey Carmichael, his latest patient, would say about all this. She'd probably think she'd stepped into a fairytale with music and dancing... and gorgeous princes and princesses. She, as well as a lot of other children, was in dire need of the care the money raised would provide.

His lips curved as he thought about that morning when he'd carried the tiny four-year-old into the OR. Bright, sweet and with an adorable lisp, she'd wrapped her arms around his neck and planted a kiss on his cheek.

Lifting a hand, he was surprised not to feel the damp spot her lips had left and his heart ached for the brave little girl who'd cheerfully told everyone who'd listened that Mr. Doctor was going to make her beautiful again.

Fortunately she was still very young and the trauma of being savaged by a friend's pet would fade, along with her scars.

When Holly's mother had called him last week to urge him to attend the ball, he'd told himself that he'd accepted for Lacey. He'd lied to himself. It was also a chance for him to get Holly alone and…

And what?

Apologize? Bare his soul? Force another kiss on her? He didn't know. Only this afternoon he'd looked into huge blue eyes full of hurt and pride and had known one irrefutable fact: he loved Holly Buchanan more than he'd thought it possible to love another person.

It had left him reeling, totally off balance, like the world had spun off its axis. Like he'd been head-punched by a linebacker. Hell, he was still reeling. Or maybe he'd always been a little off center and Holly just…righted his world. Made everything better. Brighter, sweeter… Hell…it had sounded sappy and a little goofy even thinking about it.

But this bizarre feeling growing inside his chest had had his emotions seesawing between elation and pure terror. It had left him feeling shaky and sick. And then he'd heard that Holly had talked to Dr. Hunt about taking up a fellowship in another city and the sick feeling had morphed into outright panic.

She was planning to leave—because she thought he preferred Paige. As if anyone, especially that spoiled shallow supermodel, could ever make him feel the way Holly did.

Suddenly the thought of being without her had filled him with a determination born of fear. A fear he'd shoved aside with the knowledge that if she didn't care about him—even a little—she wouldn't be thinking of ditching her plan. Or him.

He was going to make her listen and he was going to do it tonight. And then he was going to take her home and tie her to his bed.

Fingering the invitation Delia had delivered to the hospital, he recalled the neatly penned instructions on the back.

Gabriel. Table 1 to the right of the dais. 7:30. Don't be late or I'll send out a search party. Delia.

He checked the seating plan on the easel at the entrance and headed across the dance floor. The live orchestra, all students from the Manhattan Music College, filled the ballroom with lively music, proving that Delia Buchanan supported young talent as well as raised funds for the dis-figured.

She was a remarkable woman, he thought. Just like her daughter.

He skirted a group of people sipping champagne and de-bating the safety of air travel when a familiar voice purred behind him, "You all alone tonight, Gabriel?"

He didn't have to turn around to know that Paige Bu-chanan was on the prowl.

"No, actually," he said, turning to find a stunningly made-up Paige clinging to the arm of the man she'd not two weeks ago said was a dead bore.

"Ms. Buchanan, Westchester." He greeted the other man blandly but he guessed his feelings were pretty clear because Richard Westchester's brown eyes twinkled as he thrust out his hand in greeting.

"Alexander." His handshake was firm. "If you're looking for Holly, I saw her talking to the senator and Mrs. James over at the auction table."

A senator? "Thank you." He was just about to head off when Rick tilted his head, studying Gabe with narrowed eyes.

"You know, you remind me of someone. I thought so the other night but I just couldn't think who it was. Seeing you again has reminded me. Are you by any chance related to the Long Island Alexanders? Mark Alexander's son, Ste-ven, is about your age, maybe a little younger, and you look a lot like him."

Gabe had known this moment would eventually come. Had prepared for it. But it still gave him a jolt. "No," he said casually. "I'm from California."

"Oh, that's right," Rick mused. "Funny how life is. I

guess it's true what they say about having a twin some-where in the world."

Gabe was saved from replying by Paige. Clearly tired of being ignored, she tugged impatiently on Rick's arm. "Come on, Ricky." She pouted. "I want to show you the dresses I donated to my mother's little pet project."

"The auction," Rick said, by way of explanation to Gabe, who couldn't have cared less unless they brought in a lot of money.

"I'm sure the foundation is grateful for your loss," Gabe said politely. Paige sent him a cat smile.

"And you, Gabriel?" she purred. "How grateful are you? Considering most of the funds will be going to pay for your salary?"

"God, Paige," Rick groaned. "Give it a rest, will you? You know very well that Chrysalis can't afford to pay Dr. Alexander's fees. Anything made here tonight only goes to the medical costs for the miracles he performs."

Furious with Rick for daring to contradict her in front of Gabriel, she rounded on him. "I'm only saying—"

"Yeah, yeah," Rick interrupted wearily. "We get it. The great Paige Buchanan threw a couple of her old rags at the foundation and now everyone must be overcome with grati-tude. You're thirty-one years old, for God's sake. Don't you think it's time you stopped behaving like a spoiled brat?"

"I am not that old," she whispered furiously, two spots of color appearing high on her famous cheekbones.

Rick sighed. "We're the same age, Paige, and I'm thirty-one. Almost thirty-two, in fact, which means—"

"I know what it means, Rick. It means you're an insen-sitive jerk and I never should have agreed to come with you tonight."

"No one else would bring you," he said brutally, to which she replied by sending him a look that should have sliced him to shreds before spinning on her heel and flouncing off.

After a short silence Rick shoved a hand through his

hair. "Sorry about that. The thing is…" He let his breath out in a long hiss. "I've been in love with Paige since I was six." He gave a hard laugh. "And you can see just how that worked out for me."

Gabe was confused. "If you're in love with Paige," he asked, "then what the hell was that display with Holly the other night?"

A dull flush rose up Rick's neck. "My pathetic attempt to make Paige jealous." He gave an embarrassed laugh. "I thought you'd arrived with Paige and…and ended up embarrassing myself. Look, Holly's the best, but Paige? Well, it's always been Paige for me."

Gabe understood because he had a feeling it would always be Holly for him. "My condolences."

Rick's laugh burst out and he grimaced. "Thanks. And now I think I'll just go drown my sorrows. Coming?"

He shook his head. "I need to speak to Holly."

"Hope you have better luck," Rick muttered.

After he left, Gabe spotted Holly across the ballroom and sucked in a hard breath at the picture she made; slender and stunning in a long column of ice blue that complemented her dark hair…and deepened the blue of her eyes.

She looked both touchable and as distant as a star, and she literally took his breath away. The one-sleeved dress was a feat of engineering that hugged and draped her curves before falling to the floor in a luxurious cascade of soft folds from an artfully draped row of fabric blossoms at her hip. It was at once modest and incredibly revealing, and while it cleverly covered her scarred right arm it exposed her flawless shoulder and arm entirely.

He didn't realize he'd been standing there staring at her like a lovesick schoolboy until someone bumped into him, jolting him out of his trance. With his eyes on her, he murmured an apology and started forward.

She must have sensed his stare because she looked up and their gazes locked. It was like one of those sappy movie moments when two people locked eyes across a crowded room. Everything faded—the people, the noise, the opulence—until there was only the two of them.

After a few heated beats a tentative smile trembled on her lips and warmth filled him, rising in his chest like bubbles in a champagne glass. Her gaze dropped to the dimple in his cheek and he realized he was smiling too.

Oh, yeah, he thought, she couldn't resist his dimples. Or his kisses. He just hoped she listened to what he had to say.

"Oh, Gabriel," a low feminine voice came from behind him. "I'm so glad you made it."

CHAPTER THIRTEEN

GABRIEL TURNED TO find Delia Buchanan at his elbow and wasn't the least bit surprised when she cupped his face in her hands studied him for a few beats before reaching up to kiss his cheek.

"Good evening, Mrs. Buchanan. *Wow.* You look amazing." She wore a simple off-the-shoulder black jersey dress only a true blonde could pull off.

"Oh, darn." She laughed up at him. "I was hoping the best-looking man in the room would call me by my name and make all the other women jealous."

Gabe smiled and kissed her cheek. "You're the most beautiful woman here, Delia," he murmured, his gaze sliding to Holly, who was watching them with an odd expression on her face. A kind of hopeful yearning that grabbed him by the throat and tugged him toward her. "After your daughter, of course."

She squeezed his arm. "And you're incredibly sweet, Gabriel. I only hope she knows how lucky she is."

"I'm the lucky one," he said, watching as color blossomed beneath Holly's skin. "Or I will be when I finally corner her and—"

She gasped softly, looking stunned and desperately hopeful. "Oh…oh, my…you're in love with her."

Gabe felt the back of his neck grow hot and grimaced. "It's that obvious?"

A lovely smile transformed her features and he caught his breath at how very much alike Holly and her mother were. "Only to a mother who's been waiting for this moment for a long, long time," she said on a rush of emotion. "For someone to love her enough to overlook the scars."

"She's beautiful," he murmured, taking in Holly's creamy skin, heavily lashed eyes and the tendrils of dark hair framing her oval face. "Inside and out." He turned to Delia. "Like her mother."

Tears filled her eyes and her breath hitched audibly. "Oh, you." She pressed her hand into the center of her chest and blinked a few times. She gave a soft sniff. "Look what you've done now. You've made me all weepy."

Gabriel felt his skull tighten. The last thing he'd wanted was to upset Holly's mother. Not tonight. Not ever. He shoved unsteady fingers through his hair and looked around for an escape route but there wasn't one.

Maybe he should have taken Westchester up on that drink after all. "Oh, man, I'm…sorry. Can I get you anything? Water, champagne? *Anything?*"

Delia laughed tearfully as she nudged his shoulder and he realized he'd started to sound desperate there for a second. "Look at you, getting all panicky over a few tears," she hiccuped. "Besides, what's a little smudged mascara when someone loves my baby?"

Embarrassed, Gabe rubbed the back of his neck and shifted his feet, feeling fifteen again. "Yeah, well," he said, clearing his throat. "Maybe I should see if she'll forgive me for being a colossal ass first."

"Oh, before you do," Delia said, as though she'd suddenly remembered. "There's someone I want you to meet first. He's a huge contributor to both the hospital and the foundation." She slipped her hand into the crook of his elbow and urged him forward. "In fact, he's responsible for the planned expansion of the P&R wing. And if I'm not mistaken, he was also instrumental in getting you here."

Gabe reluctantly allowed her to pull him forward. "Me?"

"Oh, yes," she said with a lovely smile. "We only wanted the best for the program. In fact, the endowment depended on you heading up the team."

Gabriel frowned and wondered at the sudden bad feeling in his stomach. "That's a bit harsh. I'm sure there are other surgeons who could have filled the position."

"They wanted the best and apparently that's you." She squeezed his arm and sent him a proud smile. "Here we are," she said brightly, reaching out to touch the shoulder of a much older man who had his back to them.

When he turned, Gabe's blood froze.

Through the dull roaring in his ears he heard Delia Buchanan say, "Mr. Alexander, I'd like to introduce you to the hospital's newest acquisition. He's already made a huge difference to some of our recipients." As though she'd felt the instant Gabe's muscles turn to stone, she flicked him a concerned look before including the other members of the group.

"This is Dr. Al...ex...an...der?" Her eyes widened as enlightenment slowly dawned. She gave a shocked gasp, her gaze whipping up to his—looking suddenly shaken and distressed. "Oh." She lifted a trembling hand to her chest. "Oh, Gabriel, I'm so sorry."

As though Gabe's worlds weren't suddenly colliding, Caspar Alexander took Delia's hand and pressed a kiss to her cheek. "You're looking more radiant than ever, my dear. And the ballroom's never looked better." Then he straightened and turned his cold blue eyes on Gabriel.

He didn't offer his hand—probably because Gabe looked ready to take a bite of anything that moved. "Gabriel," he said smoothly. "You're looking well."

Gabe's reply, "Sir," as frigid as the north wind, slid like an icy blade into the sudden silence. He ignored the shocked expressions around him as he zeroed in on Mark Alexander, looking as stunned as Delia Buchanan. She tightened her fingers on his arm and pressed closer to his side as though she instinctively knew what was happening and was offering her silent support.

And Gabriel, grateful for her warm maternal presence, fell in love for the second time that day. He covered the hand gripping his arm and gave it a reassuring squeeze.

"Hello, Dad," he said with a blade-sharp smile. "Long time no see." And had the satisfaction of seeing Mark Alexander turn white. As though Mark had seen a ghost—or maybe his past coming up to bite him in the ass. And though Gabe wanted to hate him, he realized Mark was as stunned as the rest of the Alexander clan. A quick glance at Caspar showed the old man looking pleased, as though he'd orchestrated the events for maximum shock value.

Clearly Caspar wasn't done controlling his family. But Gabriel wasn't family and he had no intention of being manipulated by anyone. Especially the old bastard.

Oh, wait, he thought savagely. *He* was the unwanted son. *He* was the long "lost" grandson Caspar wanted to pull into his web of lies, deceit and tight-fisted control. He hadn't managed to bribe Gabe with riches and power three years ago so he'd gone for the jugular. He'd bought Gabe the one thing he'd needed after his mother's death—to do something worthwhile. To help people who really needed it, not just because they could afford to pay for their vanity.

The expression on her mother's face sent Holly's pulse ratcheting up a couple of thousand notches. Something was wrong, she thought, murmuring an excuse to Senator James and his wife. Seriously wrong.

Gabriel, looking coldly furious, appeared to have been

turned to stone but it was the distress on her mother's face and the way she clutched at his arm that had Holly moving quickly toward them.

She recognized the old man facing her and if she wondered what Caspar Alexander had said to make Gabriel so mad, she arrived just as he turned to his son with a coldly satisfied smile.

"Mark," he said airily. "Meet your son. Steven, Jade and Courtney, meet your brother. *Dr.* Gabriel Alexander." Holly's gasp was drowned out by other shocked gasps around them. Gleefully enjoying the drama, Caspar turned to Gabriel and with a gesture of disgust he said, "Son, meet your family."

Holly froze, her eyes locked on the frozen tableau before her. Gabriel had stiffened even more until the air vibrated with tension.

"You don't get to call me son," he said quietly, lethally. "You don't get to call me anything. You gave up that right the night you tried to force my mother to have an abortion."

Holly's horrified gasp covered her mother's soft moan and she grabbed Delia's hand and squeezed. The ballroom had gone ominously quiet and people were beginning to stare.

And to Holly's shock, instead of denying the claim, Caspar just snorted derisively. "I did you a favor, boy," he said. "Look at you. You're a self-made man. If I hadn't, you might have ended up just like them." He waved a whiskey-filled glass.

"Father?" Mark Alexander asked faintly, looking alarmingly pale. "Is that true? You threatened Rachel? You told me she'd lost the baby. You told me she'd moved west to get over the loss. How could you do this? I did everything you asked of me."

"Yes, you did." The old man nodded, casually lifting the whiskey tumbler to his lips. "Maybe I would have respected you more if you'd defied me. Maybe these blood-sucking offspring of yours would have grown up to be more like Gabriel. More like me."

"I'm nothing like you," Gabriel snarled.

"Oh, yes, you are," Caspar interrupted. "You wouldn't have dragged yourself up from the gutter if you weren't."

Gabriel looked like he was contemplating murder. "I did it for my mother, not for you."

"I was wrong," Caspar said, but Holly's gaze was locked on Mark's face and knew the instant he was in trouble. "Rachel Parker was a fine woman, and a good mother. Look how well you—"

"Gabriel, your father—" Holly began, stepping toward the older man, who was clutching his chest and starting to buckle. Gabriel, quickly assessing the situation, leapt forward, catching Mark before he fell.

"Mom," Holly murmured. "Call 911." She dropped to her knees beside the gray and gasping man. "Gabriel, I'll do it," she began, placing her hands on Mark's chest to begin CPR, but Gabriel brushed her aside.

He pulled his father into a sitting position and thumped him hard on the back. "Cough," he said sharply. "And hard, like you've got something in your throat."

Holly's gaze snapped up. "What—?" Of course. "He's right, Mr. Alexander, cough really hard." Mark looked at them like they were crazy. "Please," Holly said, her eyes filling with tears. "It'll get your heart beating properly again."

Her encouragement worked and with Gabriel's help Mark started coughing, a little feebly at first, then harder until his color gradually returned.

Holly sat back, her eyes locked on Gabriel's face. He'd had every right to turn and walk away—had had every opportunity—yet he hadn't. And here he was, saving the man who hadn't been there for his mother. Hadn't been there for him.

As though sensing her gaze, Gabriel suddenly looked up

and their eyes locked. The stark fear and desperate hope in them nearly crushed Holly and it was in that moment she realized the naked truth.

She was in love with him and she would do anything— anything—to help him through this.

"I'll get some brandy," she said, and rose to her feet.

CHAPTER FOURTEEN

HOLLY PAUSED OUTSIDE the hospital room, her gaze riveted on Gabriel's broad back and the rumpled sun-streaked hair that appeared even more rumpled than usual.

She wanted more than anything to go to him and smooth the unruly locks that tended to flop onto his forehead but her heart was hammering against her ribs and she was still struggling to catch her breath after dashing halfway across the island.

Okay, she'd only dashed a few blocks, but in four-inch glittery heels and a long snug evening gown it was a miracle she hadn't broken her neck.

Her heart now, well, that was another matter altogether, especially when it gave a sharp wrench at the picture he made, silhouetted against the darkened sky. Her breath caught in her throat.

Oh, God. He looked so lonely and solitary…as if the weight of the universe rested on his broad shoulders. And suddenly she wanted to go to him, rest her head against his broad back and give him what he needed.

With his back to the room, and hands buried deep in the pockets of his tux pants, he faced the darkened window overlooking the lights of Manhattan. At any other time the view might have distracted Holly, but her attention was riveted on his tense back and the I-want-to-be-alone aura he'd wrapped around himself like an invisible cloak.

She'd returned to find Mark recovering nicely but planning to return to their room. There'd been no sign of Gabriel but she'd known instinctively where to find him.

"You shouldn't be here, Holly," he said quietly.

"Why not?" she asked, just as quietly, her heart suddenly aching with the realization she'd made a short while ago. She'd suspected she was in love after her father's birthday but she'd hoped it was just a little crush. Hoped it would fade with time. It hadn't. Wouldn't…ever.

"You said we needed to talk."

He gave a ragged laugh. "Really? You want to talk now?"

She stepped into the room. "It's quiet, we're alone. What better time?"

"I made a mistake." His voice was so low and ragged in the quiet room that she strained to hear the words that seemed to be wrenched from a place of deep pain. The suppressed emotion in it drew her across the room.

"With what?" she asked, joining him at the window.

He sighed heavily. "Coming here. You."

Oh. Her breath caught at the unexpected shaft of pain his words sent lancing through her heart. And she knew in that instant how it would feel—as though her heart was being ripped from her chest and crushed. "You…" She gulped. "You can't mean that?"

"Yes," he asserted, sounding unbearably weary. "I do. I knew I should stay away from you but now…" He sent her a brief glance.

"Now…what?"

He shook his head. "I can't imagine that you would want to have anything to do with me. Not now."

Her eyes widened and she licked her lips. "What do you mean?"

"You heard me, Holly." He gave a short laugh. "Hell, the entire ballroom heard me."

Holly was confused. Yes, she'd heard him but couldn't remember him saying anything to be ashamed of. "You mean when you called your grandfather a ruthless war-lord who didn't deserve to breathe the same air as the rest of humanity?"

He snorted out a laugh. "Yeah, that would be it."

She was silent for a couple of beats. "Is that the truth? Did he pay your mother to have an abortion?"

"Yeah. Pretty much. Although it apparently went more along the lines of 'If you don't take care of it the next person I send will make sure that thing doesn't survive another week' kind of thing."

"Well, then, the shame's on him, isn't it?" She bumped his shoulder with hers. "I'm glad your mother didn't take his money." She sent him a warm smile. "It showed guts. She must be awesome. I can see where you get it from."

His somber expression lightened. "She was. A real fighter. She lost the fight to cancer a few months ago."

She faced him now. "Oh, Gabriel, I'm so sorry. Is that… when you decided to move east?"

He frowned and Holly could see the subject change upset him. A muscle in his jaw flexed. "I got a letter from West Manhattan offering me my own team of top surgeons, prom-ises of unlimited funds and the most up-to-date technol-ogy in the best teaching hospital in the world." He barked out a hard laugh. "I was flattered. I couldn't believe they'd chosen me to—"

He broke off with a muttered oath and turned away, fist-ing both hands as though he was controlling himself with effort. But she'd seen the fury and humiliation burning in his blue-green gaze and her heart broke for him. She could un-derstand what it would do to such a proud, determined man.

"Do you have any idea how humiliating it is to find out that I was forced onto Langley, onto Hunt?" he demanded.

"Oh, Gabriel. My mother's devastated that she said any-thing. She didn't know. She would never do anything like that knowingly."

"It's not Delia's fault I handled it so badly." He shifted

his shoulders as though to loosen some of the tension there. "I can't think what she must think of me."

"My mother said if she was twenty years younger, she'd divorce my father and marry you herself."

He laughed and Holly's heart lifted at the sound, even though it was ragged and a bit rusty. "Yeah." His dimple emerged, distracting her from his next words. "I think I love your mother." And when they finally penetrated the jumble of emotion swamping her, she blinked.

"You...do?"

"How could I not?" he demanded. "When she's so much like her daughter."

Her heart stuttered and the fragile hope that had been slowly blooming in her chest shriveled. "What...what are you saying? Paige?"

"No, Holly," he said gently, taking her by the shoulders and turning her so she faced him. "*Not* Paige. You."

Her world tilted and swam, forcing her to blink up at him or pass out from shock. "M-me?" she stuttered, breaking off to swallow the rusty squeak emerging from her tight throat.

A half-smile teased his lips but his eyes were intense, watchful. "Yeah," he said firmly. "You."

"But I'm...you're—"

"I'm what? You're what?" he asked, when she continued to splutter and stare at him as though he'd suggested she jump from the window.

"Look at me, Gabriel. I'm...and you're..." She stopped because she was beginning to stutter and hyperventilate like she used to as a child.

"You're not making sense, Holly. Take a deep breath and try again."

Holly breathed in and then out a few times till the urge to pass out faded, staring at him silently for a few moments before gesturing to the window.

"Tell me what you see," she said quietly, her pulse hammering in her throat.

He searched her expression before turning to stare at their reflection in the window. "I see a beautiful woman with a soft heart and a quick mind. A woman who isn't afraid to face the world, even with her scars." He turned to stare down into her face. "I see a woman who's a little clumsy at times but only when she's flustered. And I kind of like that I'm the only one who makes her nervous." He drew in a deep breath and turned away. His next words were low and hoarse. "I see a woman who's too good for a man like me."

She blinked. "Wha—?"

"I'm the dirty little secret, Holly. Isn't that what this mess is all about? Caspar Alexander's unwanted grandson causing a scandal on your mother's big night?"

"*No!* How can you say that?"

"It doesn't matter, because I've decided to go back to California."

"You…you have?"

He sighed. "Yeah. It's best."

"For whom?"

He looked startled. "For you, of course. I would never humiliate you or your mother. My staying does that."

"Don't be an ass," Holly snapped, suddenly so furious she wanted to punch Caspar Alexander for what he'd done to Gabriel. And she wanted to punch Gabriel too; for letting the old man control his life. "That's just your pride talking."

"What are you talking about? I have no pride left. I accepted the position at West Manhattan because I thought they wanted *me*…not the Alexander money."

Frustrated, Holly grabbed his shirt and yanked him close until they were nose to nose. "I've seen you work, Gabriel. I've heard people talk about what you've done. The amazing techniques you've pioneered and not with vain, shallow women looking for bigger boobs or thinner thighs. But there…" She gestured wildly to the small bed holding a sleeping child. "Where a little girl disfigured by a dog attack is telling everyone that you're going to make her beautiful again. Or…or a man looking to rebuild his shattered face and self-esteem."

She drew in a shuddery breath. "That," she said fervently, smoothing her hands over the creases she'd made in his shirt front. "That's why you're here. Not because of the Alexander money." She looked into his stunned face. "Don't you see? We need you here. They need you here."

After a long pause, Gabriel asked softly, "And you, Holly? What do you need?"

"I…" She felt a shaft of panic go through her when he continued to stare at her, waiting. She sucked in air and took the plunge. "I…" She gulped. "I need you too."

"Oh, boy," he said, looking stunned and relieved and terrified all at once. His reaction confused her and she stumbled back a step but he gave a ragged laugh and yanked her close, wrapping his arms around her so she couldn't escape.

"Say it," he ordered, the expression in his eyes making her knees weak. Her eyes dropped to his mouth.

"Wha-at?"

"Say it."

She licked her lips nervously. "You…first."

His mouth curled up at one corner and his eyes shimmered with tenderness. "God, is it any wonder I love you as much as I do?"

Holly gasped as shock and happiness burst inside her head like a meteor shower. "I…uh, what did you say?"

He laughed and pressed a quick kiss to her mouth. "You heard me. I said—"

"I thought you were in love with my mother," she said breathlessly.

"No," he said with a chuckle. "I said I love your mother." He gazed at her for a long moment, his eyes touching on every inch of her face as though he was committing her face to memory. "It's you I'm in love with. Only you."

"Oh," Holly said, tears filling her eyes at the emotion blazing in his. "You're sure?"

He chuckled. "How could I not be?" He tucked her closer and bent to kiss her mouth tenderly. "You threw yourself at my feet; gave me a lap dance I'll never forget and tried to drown yourself to get my attention." He dropped a smiling kiss on her intricate hairdo when she gave an embarrassed groan and hid her face against his throat. After a few beats he cupped her neck and drew her back so he could look into her eyes.

"Every time you fell at my feet I was the one falling until there was no getting up from what you make me feel."

Her breath hitched. "I...I... *Oh!*"

"Say you love me, Holly. Say you'll stay in Manhattan and build a future with me."

She grimaced at the reminder that she'd discussed her plans to apply for a fellowship in another city. "You heard that?"

"Yes, and it sent me into a panic." He gave her a quick shake. "Now. Your turn."

For long moments she studied the face of the hottest man in Manhattan and decided that she'd never curse her clumsiness again. It had, after all, landed her at Gabriel's feet and she knew without asking that he'd always be there to catch her.

She lifted her hands to cup his cheeks. "I love you," she said, rising onto her toes and sealing the words with a kiss. "Always."

* * * * *

MILLS & BOON®
Hardback – September 2015

ROMANCE

The Greek Commands His Mistress	Lynne Graham
A Pawn in the Playboy's Game	Cathy Williams
Bound to the Warrior King	Maisey Yates
Her Nine Month Confession	Kim Lawrence
Traded to the Desert Sheikh	Caitlin Crews
A Bride Worth Millions	Chantelle Shaw
Vows of Revenge	Dani Collins
From One Night to Wife	Rachael Thomas
Reunited by a Baby Secret	Michelle Douglas
A Wedding for the Greek Tycoon	Rebecca Winters
Beauty & Her Billionaire Boss	Barbara Wallace
Newborn on Her Doorstep	Ellie Darkins
Falling at the Surgeon's Feet	Lucy Ryder
One Night in New York	Amy Ruttan
Daredevil, Doctor...Husband?	Alison Roberts
The Doctor She'd Never Forget	Annie Claydon
Reunited...in Paris!	Sue MacKay
French Fling to Forever	Karin Baine
Claimed	Tracy Wolff
Maid for a Magnate	Jules Bennett

0815 GEN STD HB

MILLS & BOON®
Large Print – September 2015

ROMANCE

The Sheikh's Secret Babies	Lynne Graham
The Sins of Sebastian Rey-Defoe	Kim Lawrence
At Her Boss's Pleasure	Cathy Williams
Captive of Kadar	Trish Morey
The Marakaios Marriage	Kate Hewitt
Craving Her Enemy's Touch	Rachael Thomas
The Greek's Pregnant Bride	Michelle Smart
The Pregnancy Secret	Cara Colter
A Bride for the Runaway Groom	Scarlet Wilson
The Wedding Planner and the CEO	Alison Roberts
Bound by a Baby Bump	Ellie Darkins

HISTORICAL

A Lady for Lord Randall	Sarah Mallory
The Husband Season	Mary Nichols
The Rake to Reveal Her	Julia Justiss
A Dance with Danger	Jeannie Lin
Lucy Lane and the Lieutenant	Helen Dickson

MEDICAL

Baby Twins to Bind Them	Carol Marinelli
The Firefighter to Heal Her Heart	Annie O'Neil
Tortured by Her Touch	Dianne Drake
It Happened in Vegas	Amy Ruttan
The Family She Needs	Sue MacKay
A Father for Poppy	Abigail Gordon

MILLS & BOON®
Hardback – October 2015

ROMANCE

Claimed for Makarov's Baby	Sharon Kendrick
An Heir Fit for a King	Abby Green
The Wedding Night Debt	Cathy Williams
Seducing His Enemy's Daughter	Annie West
Reunited for the Billionaire's Legacy	Jennifer Hayward
Hidden in the Sheikh's Harem	Michelle Conder
Resisting the Sicilian Playboy	Amanda Cinelli
The Return of Antonides	Anne McAllister
Soldier, Hero...Husband?	Cara Colter
Falling for Mr December	Kate Hardy
The Baby Who Saved Christmas	Alison Roberts
A Proposal Worth Millions	Sophie Pembroke
The Baby of Their Dreams	Carol Marinelli
Falling for Her Reluctant Sheikh	Amalie Berlin
Hot-Shot Doc, Secret Dad	Lynne Marshall
Father for Her Newborn Baby	Lynne Marshall
His Little Christmas Miracle	Emily Forbes
Safe in the Surgeon's Arms	Molly Evans
Pursued	Tracy Wolff
A Royal Temptation	Charlene Sands

MILLS & BOON®
Large Print – October 2015

ROMANCE

The Bride Fonseca Needs	Abby Green
Sheikh's Forbidden Conquest	Chantelle Shaw
Protecting the Desert Heir	Caitlin Crews
Seduced into the Greek's World	Dani Collins
Tempted by Her Billionaire Boss	Jennifer Hayward
Married for the Prince's Convenience	Maya Blake
The Sicilian's Surprise Wife	Tara Pammi
His Unexpected Baby Bombshell	Soraya Lane
Falling for the Bridesmaid	Sophie Pembroke
A Millionaire for Cinderella	Barbara Wallace
From Paradise...to Pregnant!	Kandy Shepherd

HISTORICAL

A Mistress for Major Bartlett	Annie Burrows
The Chaperon's Seduction	Sarah Mallory
Rake Most Likely to Rebel	Bronwyn Scott
Whispers at Court	Blythe Gifford
Summer of the Viking	Michelle Styles

MEDICAL

Just One Night?	Carol Marinelli
Meant-To-Be Family	Marion Lennox
The Soldier She Could Never Forget	Tina Beckett
The Doctor's Redemption	Susan Carlisle
Wanted: Parents for a Baby!	Laura Iding
His Perfect Bride?	Louisa Heaton

MILLS & BOON®

Why shop at millsandboon.co.uk?

Each year, thousands of romance readers find their perfect read at millsandboon.co.uk. That's because we're passionate about bringing you the very best romantic fiction. Here are some of the advantages of shopping at www.millsandboon.co.uk:

* **Get new books first**—you'll be able to buy your favourite books one month before they hit the shops

* **Get exclusive discounts**—you'll also be able to buy our specially created monthly collections, with up to 50% off the RRP

* **Find your favourite authors**—latest news, interviews and new releases for all your favourite authors and series on our website, plus ideas for what to try next

* **Join in**—once you've bought your favourite books, don't forget to register with us to rate, review and join in the discussions

Visit **www.millsandboon.co.uk**
for all this and more today!